the angels of mona terrace

the angels of mona terrace

Steve Wood

Priory Press

First published 2009

ISBN 978-0-9551510-5-7

Although this book is set in and around Manchester and the Isle of Man the characters are fictional and any similarity to anyone living or dead is simply coincidence and the product of the author's extraordinarily vivid imagination.

Photograph by Victoria Harrop
www.manxphotography.com

Edited and typeset by
Frances Hackeson Freelance Publishing Services,
Brinscall, Lancs
Printed in Great Britain by Bell and Bain Ltd, Glasgow

Have you ever played a game called Buccaneer? Each player has a little galleon and has to sail to Treasure Island to collect gold and diamonds and things. Then you have to make good speed to your home port before anybody attacks your ship and makes off with your booty. Mum got it from the church jumble sale for my birthday. A couple of rubies are missing otherwise it's in really good nick.

I took it to school on the last day of term – we're always allowed to play games on the final day. If somebody had told me then that during the holiday I really would be sailing to a faraway island, I'd have laughed. At the time I'd never been out of Manchester. Buccaneer was the closest I'd been to the sea!

If they'd tried to tell me the island was a secret place where people go after they've died, I'd have thought they were nuts. And if they went on to say I'd be staying there in a house run by a family of angels I would have smiled politely and waited for the men in white coats to come and take them away.

But that's what really happened. I want to tell everybody about it, but perhaps I'm supposed to keep it hushed up. So I've decided to write it all down in a notebook. Everything. When I've finished I'm going to bury the book in my time capsule and leave it to chance. It might never be found and nobody will ever know. But, if you're reading this, it **has** been found and my story can be told.

I'm writing it in September 1971. I wonder when you're reading it. It really doesn't matter when, I just want to tell you all about it ...

chapter 1

Owen, Neville and Billy had never played Buccaneer before. Ten minutes into the game Owen realised he was going to lose. His ship had been blown off course and his crew washed overboard and lost at sea. He hid the dice until we agreed to play a game called Consequences that his big sister plays with her mates.

He wrote something down on a piece of paper, folded it over and gave it to Neville. Neville wrote something down, folded it over and passed it to Billy. When we'd all had a go, Owen read the story. He wasn't using his normal voice – he was doing an impression of Mr Heath. (The headmaster, not the Prime Minister.) Billy was having hysterics and Neville was laughing so much I thought he was going to throw up.

'What's going on?' said Miss Stern.

We stopped laughing immediately. None of us spoke, but I was holding the piece of paper with the story on it – Owen had shoved it into my hand at the first sign of trouble.

'Would you like to read that to the whole class, Samuel? Then we can all share the joke.'

'No, miss.'

'I beg your pardon?'

'I mean, no miss, I – '

'Read it out, please.'

My hands were shaking. So was my voice. 'Mr Heath met Miss Stern.'

There were a few giggles from the back of the class-room.

'He said … he said … '

'Carry on, Samuel.'

'He said … I fancy you.'

Some of the girls screamed.

'She said … my knickers are too tight.'

Some of the boys sniggered.

'And the consequence was … they snogged in the bushes.'

Everybody went mad – laughing and screaming and banging on the tables. It was the biggest riot since Joseph fell off the stage during the Nativity play.

'Quiet! Whose idea was this?'

I looked at Owen. His stare said 'just you dare'.

I shrugged my shoulders.

Miss Stern was fuming. 'Go and stand in the corner! If you're going to behave like one of the infants, that's how you'll be treated!'

She made me stay behind at home time and put the chairs on the tables. It was Owen's fault. He caused the trouble, but I got the blame. Typical.

He was waiting for me at the school gates with Neville and Billy. Barney was there too.

Barney's my little brother. He follows me everywhere and copies everything I do – it's really annoying. I once told Mum about it and she gave me one of her 'serious' talks. She sat me down and told me I was very lucky to have a little brother and I should look after him. I told her that Matt never looks after *me* and I'm *his* little brother. (She had no answer to that.)

Barney was holding a model he'd made in Arts and Crafts. For months he'd been taking the inside of toilet rolls to school and now he'd stuck them together and painted them green. I asked him what it was supposed to be.

'It's a dragon, what does it look like?'

'It looks like a giant bogey.'

'Get lost.'

'Get lost yourself.'

On the way home Owen said he was going to take a shortcut down the alley near Hemmons Road. None of us are supposed to go down there because that's where the man was arrested for playing hopscotch in his underpants.

Owen set off with Billy and Neville hot on his heels. I knew I'd never hear the last of it if I chickened out so I took a deep breath and followed. I walked as quickly as I could without breaking into a run. Barney trotted along behind. The alley was a mess and it stank – all the dustbins had been pushed over and rubbish was scattered all over the cobbles.

Suddenly a man appeared at one of the back gates. We stopped dead in our tracks.

'What are you lot doing?' he said.

None of us spoke.

'What school do you go to?'

Silence.

'What school do you go to?' he shouted.

'Crowcroft Park,' said Neville.

'Right,' said the man. 'I'm going to go and see the headmaster and tell him you boys pushed all these dustbins over.'

'I know what he'll say,' said Owen. 'What a load of rubbish!'

'Cheeky little beggar!'

Owen started running. Billy and Neville sprinted after him with me bringing up the rear. Barney didn't move – he was glued to the spot.

'Sam!' he screamed. 'Don't leave me!'

I ran back to him, grabbed him by the scruff of the neck and dragged him up the alley – his feet hardly touched the ground. The dragon couldn't stand the pace – green cardboard tubes bounced along behind us.

We didn't tell Mum what had happened in the alley – she would have been disappointed. I didn't tell her I'd been in trouble with Miss Stern – she would have felt let down.

If ever we did anything wrong Mum would say she was disappointed or we'd let her down, but she never lost her temper with us. She wasn't even annoyed after she'd been killed. If being dead doesn't make her angry I don't suppose anything will.

chapter 2

'I'm drowning! I'm drowning!'

Mum was washing our hair in the kitchen sink. Some of the water had gone up my nose and into my mouth.

'I can't breathe!'

Matt whacked me on the back of my legs with a towel.

'Hurry up, you big baby!' he growled. 'The water'll be frozen by the time I get a go! Why do I always have to go last anyway?'

'Because you've got the biggest nits!'

'Shut your cake hole!'

Mum told him off. 'How many times have I asked you not to talk like that, Matthew?'

I told her to wash his mouth out with soap and water. 'That's what Miss Stern did to one of the girls in our class when she swore. She took her to the loo and shoved soap suds in her mouth.'

'I'd have told her to sud off,' said Matt.

Mum warned him again. 'Any more talk like that and I *will* wash your mouth out.'

Barney shouted it at the top of his voice. 'Sud off!'

Me and Matt laughed. Mum was trying not to smile.

'I don't think it's funny,' she said. 'I've had enough of this behaviour from all three of you. Open wide!'

She grabbed a bar of soap and chased us round the

kitchen. Matt was shouting 'sud off!' and Barney was screaming. I was shaking my head from side to side, flicking water all over the place. Just then Dad came in through the back door. We all froze as if we were playing statues. He glared at Mum.

'What the hell's going on?'

Mum didn't answer.

Dad took off his coat and flung it at Matt as usual. I got his slippers out of the pantry. Dad snatched them from me, went through to the living room and slumped into his chair.

I helped Mum to mop the kitchen floor. I felt sorry for her because we'd got her into trouble. Matt must have felt sorry for her too – he went into the living room and turned the telly on really loud. He knew it would annoy Dad and it wasn't long before he got the reaction he was looking for.

'Turn that off.'

'I'm watching it.'

'Off.'

'In a minute.'

'Now!'

I didn't want any more trouble so I went in and switched it off.

I can remember what was on the TV at that exact moment – an advert for washing powder – I'll never forget it as long as I live.

'Buy now for your chance to win a family holiday!' shouted the man.

I wish he'd kept his big mouth shut. If he hadn't told me about that stupid washing powder Mum would still be alive.

We were all sitting round the table having our tea when I first mentioned it.

'Can we get some of that washing powder off the telly, Mum? We might win a holiday.'

'You need brains to win something,' said Dad. 'And you got your brains from your mother so you've no chance.' He looked at Mum. 'Isn't that right, dear?'

Mum smiled, but she didn't mean it.

'Have you ever been on holiday, Mum?' I asked.

'Not for a long time, love.'

'Owen's going on holiday,' I said. 'He's going to stay in his auntie's bungalow in Morecambe.'

'What's a bungalow?' asked Barney.

'A house with no stairs.'

'No stairs? Does that mean you never have to go to bed?'

'He reckons he's going to go in a café and have a bottle of Pepsi. Did you go in a café on holiday, Mum?'

Mum smiled and put down her knife and fork. 'I can see it as if it was yesterday. It was in a lovely spot with a huge window overlooking the sea. We went there every day, do you remember, Jack?'

Dad nodded his head without looking up from his food.

'Does it cost a lot of money to go on holiday?' I asked.

Mum nodded.

'I reckon Owen's mum and dad must be rich,' I said. 'They're going on holiday *and* they're getting a new telly. A *colour* telly!'

'What's a colour telly?' asked Barney.

'It's a new invention. All the pictures are in colour instead of black and white.'

'Wow!'

'And that's not all,' I said. 'Owen's dad is going to get a telephone put inside their house!'

'That's nothing,' said Matt. 'There's a lad at my school

who's just had a *loo* put inside his house! Imagine that! He won't have to fag down the back yard in the freezing cold every time he wants a leak.'

Barney was giggling. 'No more chilly willy.'

'Don't be silly,' said Mum. 'And eat your tea please.'

'Why have we never been on holiday, Mum?' I asked.

'We can't really afford it, love.'

'Why don't you get a job like Owen's mum? She's going to be a dinner lady.'

'You've got a job, haven't you, Mum?' said Barney. 'When you go out with your collecting boxes people give you lots of money, don't they?'

'Yes, but I don't keep it. It's for charity. Sometimes the money goes to the lifeboat organisation, sometimes it goes to the RSPCA and sometimes I collect money to help conquer cancer.'

Barney was confused. 'I didn't know conkers could get cancer.'

'Owen's dad knows somebody who works for the RSPCA,' I said. 'He's going to get Owen a guinea pig. Can we – '

'No!' snapped Dad. 'I've told you before – there are no pets coming into this house.' He pointed his knife at me. 'If I hear another word out of you, you'll be up those stairs! Owen this and Owen that, I'm sick of hearing it!' He jabbed the knife through the air as if he was stabbing me with every word. 'Do-you-un-der-stand?'

I looked at Mum. She gave me that smile. The smile that said so many things.

Don't worry, Sam, I'm here.

Don't worry, Sam, I'll never let anybody hurt you.

Don't worry, Sam, whatever happens I'll always love you.

I wanted to hug her. I wish I had. I hardly ever hugged

her. She hugged me, but I didn't hug her. That's why I was so desperate to see her again after she'd been killed. To say sorry and to give her a hug.

chapter 3

'Surprise!'

Mum gave me and Barney an empty biscuit tin. She'd got it from a coffee morning at church.

'Wow!' shrieked Barney. 'A time capsule!'

'It's brilliant!' I said. 'Thanks Mum.'

Me and Barney had been saving things to put in a time capsule ever since they made one on 'Blue Peter'. We wanted to fill it with objects that would give the people of the future an idea of life in 1971, but all we had was a Batman bubblegum card, a Colin Bell sticker (he's City's best player) and a diamond from the Buccaneer set.

(At the time, of course, I didn't know I would be writing this and adding it to our hoard. I didn't know Mum wouldn't be there to help us bury it.)

'Why don't you put an old penny in there?' said Mum. 'I think there's one in the sideboard drawer.'

'Good idea!' I said. 'When it's found it will be like ancient treasure.'

Mum dropped the penny into the biscuit tin.

'Don't tell Dad,' said Barney. 'He'll start shouting at the telly again.'

Dad got really worked up when the old money was replaced with decimal coins at the start of the year. He used to shout at Mr Heath whenever he was on the news. Dad reckoned the only reason the new coins were introduced was so that 'Heath the Thief' could put up the price of everything. When it was announced that first class stamps were going up to 3 pence each Dad went bonkers. He threw a slipper at the telly.

'Let's go and bury the time capsule,' said Barney.

'Not yet,' I said. 'We need more stuff.'

I asked Mum if she had any old photographs. She had a look in the cupboard under the stairs and pulled out an old chocolate box.

'There might be one in here you can have.'

She emptied dozens of black and white photos on to the floor. There were loads of Matt when he was a baby – smiling as if he was the sweetest thing on earth. Then he was a little boy, gazing lovingly at me, his baby brother. Next there were two boys sitting either side of baby number three, Barney.

'What do you think of this one?'

Mum was holding a photo of a man and a woman sitting on a step at the back of a house. A little girl was standing beside them.

'Is that you, Mum?' I asked.

'Yes, that's me with my mum and dad.'

Barney scratched his head. 'I never knew you had a mum and dad.'

'They died when Matthew was little.'

'Did Dad have a mum and dad?'

'Of course he did. Everybody has a mum and dad.'

'Are there any photos of them?' I asked.

'I think so,' said Mum. 'But I don't know where Dad keeps them.'

Mum handed me a photo of us three boys taken on last year's Sunday school trip.

'You can have that one if you like.'

I placed it in the biscuit tin with the rest of our treasure.

'What's this doing here?' Barney was looking at a photograph of a sailor. 'Who is it, Mum?'

'It's Dad when he was in the Navy.'

In the photo Dad's face didn't look as craggy as it does now and he had more hair. But that wasn't all.

'It doesn't look like Dad,' I said. 'He looks different.'

Then I realised why. He was smiling.

Mum took me and Barney to St Mary's Summer Fayre. On the way I told her I was worried we'd get into a fight.

'People that go to St Mary's are Catholics,' I explained. 'We're Protestants. They're always scrapping, I've seen them on the news.'

'There won't be any fighting today,' said Mum.

Barney asked why we were going and Mum said it was all about building bridges.

'One day it would be nice if people from St Mary's could feel free to come to services in our church,' she said. 'And every so often, people from our church could go to services at St Mary's.'

'What's all that got to do with the Summer Fayre?' I asked.

'We've got to start somewhere.'

Barney asked Mum if Catholics believe in Jesus.

'Of course they do.'

'Do they say prayers?'

'Yes, now keep your voice down, please.'

A man was sitting behind a table outside the church hall. Mum paid him and we stepped inside.

'Do Catholics go to heaven?' whispered Barney.

'Yes,' said Mum.

'So what's the difference?'

'There's no difference really, love. And I'm sure if each and every one of us makes a little bit of effort we can all live together as one big happy family.'

'Hannah!' A woman grabbed hold of Mum's arm. 'Thank you so much for coming.'

Mum gave us some extra pocket money to spend at the fayre while she and the woman had a natter.

Me and Barney wandered into the packed hall. Round the edges were stalls full of cakes, plants and books. Others had games. If you could throw a dart and hit a playing card you won a little toy. Barney's first dart nearly hit the woman who was running the stall.

'Mary and Joseph!' she screamed. Then she said Barney could have a prize if he promised not to throw any more darts. We went to the next stall and I tried to win a coconut. Dozens of jam jars were spread out on a table. If you could throw a ping-pong ball into one of the red jars you won. I paid for five balls and the first four missed. My last ball landed in the one gold jar in the middle of the table.

'Well done,' said the man. 'First one today.'

'Have I won? Do I get a coconut?'

'Better than that,' said the man.

He held up a plastic bag. It was full of water and swimming round in it was a little goldfish.

Me and Barney rushed to show Mum my prize. She was having a cuppa at the bar.

'I was trying to win a coconut,' I said. 'Do you think Dad will let us keep him?'

Barney was jumping up and down. 'Please! Please!'

On the way home Mum called at the pet shop and bought a small tub of fish food. She found an old fruit bowl in the kitchen cupboard, filled it with water and placed it on the sideboard. Matt poured the fish out of the plastic bag into its new home. Then he gave me and Barney our instructions.

'When Dad gets home keep your mouths shut. Don't

mention the fish. Don't even look at it.'

Barney waggled his finger in the water. 'He hasn't got a name, what shall we call him?'

'Let's call him Coconut,' I said. 'Dad said we can't have a pet, he didn't say we can't have a coconut.'

The back door opened and we all sat down and tried to look normal. Dad walked into the living room, flung his coat at Matt and sent me to fetch his slippers. Then he collapsed into his chair and Mum gave him a mug of tea. He didn't see Coconut. We knew he would see him eventually, but we all wanted that moment to be as far away as possible.

After tea Dad fell asleep as usual. Mum let us watch the telly as long as we didn't have it on too loud and wake him up. It was 'The Comedians', my favourite. One of them said he wasn't feeling very well because he'd swallowed a Christmas decoration. The doctor told him he had tinselitis.

'That's what you've got, isn't it, Sam?' said Barney.

I grabbed hold of his hair to try and shut him up. I was worried Mum had heard him and would remember about my sore throat. It had woken me up every night for a couple of weeks and she'd taken me to the doctors. He said I had to go into hospital to have my tonsils taken out. Nobody had mentioned it since and I was hoping Mum had forgotten about it.

'Sam's got tinselitis!' squeaked Barney.

'Shut it!'

I yanked his hair and he screamed. Dad woke up.

'Get to bed, you two.'

'The programme hasn't finished,' I said.

'Bed!' shouted Dad.

Barney ran over to the sideboard and kissed the fruit bowl.

'Night, night, Coconut, I love you.'

Then he realised what he'd done.

'Before you go to bed perhaps you can answer this question,' said Dad. 'What's that fish doing on the sideboard?'

'Breast stroke,' said Matt.

'I told you there were no pets coming into this house.'

'It's not a pet,' I said. 'It's a coconut, so you can't make us get rid of him.'

'It's a funny-looking coconut.'

'That's his name,' said Barney. 'He's called Coconut and he's a Catholic.'

Dad laughed. 'A what?'

'A Catholic.'

'Really?'

'Yes. And I'm sure if you make a little bit of effort we can all live together as one big happy family.'

chapter 4

I couldn't eat my cornflakes because I was so nervous. My Sunday school class was going to sing in church and I had to sing a bit on my own. It was going to be a special family service because Miss Wilmslow, the Sunday school superintendent, was retiring and Mum was going to take her place. At one point Dad said he might come (he never goes to church normally), but in the end he had the chance to do some overtime and went to work instead.

We said all the usual prayers, sang all the usual hymns and then Donald Duck gave his sermon. (Donald Duck is the vicar. His real name is Donald Cook, but us kids call him Donald Duck. Not to his face – he'd go quackers.)

He read bits from the Bible that mentioned children and then tried to explain what they meant. It was a roundabout way of talking about Sunday school and eventually he thanked Miss Wilmslow for her years of dedicated service and told her that all the children were going to miss her. (We weren't. She's about two hundred years old, she smells of mothballs and her stories go on forever.)

Donald Duck gave her a bunch of flowers and then made a speech about Mum. He said he was sure all the Sunday school children would benefit from her guidance and he knew that Mum would love them and care for them just as she does her own children.

'And now,' said Donald. 'A special musical treat.'

The dreaded moment had arrived. I followed Neville and Owen and Billy and the rest of my class to the front.

'Our very own von Trapp children will give us a rendition of "Do-Re-Mi". They will be accompanied by young Georgina on the very latest piece of musical apparatus which I am reliably informed is called a Stylophone.'

I messed it up. It was Matt's fault. When the singing started I could see him passing something to his mates. Just before it was my turn to sing, they all stuck bits of cotton wool in their ears. I missed my line and they laughed.

Donald closed the service with yet another Bible reading. He said we all have to be like children if we want to enter the kingdom of heaven and if anybody hurts any of God's children, they should have a stone put round their neck and be drowned in the sea. It didn't seem a very cheery way to end the service.

Mum had been asked to choose the final hymn. We all sang her favourite, 'What a friend we have in Jesus', during which Donald glided down the aisle and waited at the back of the church for us all to queue up and shake his hand as if he was some kind of celebrity.

Matt left with his mates. Me and Barney waited for Mum.

On the way home we walked down the alley alongside Clifton's Works. Mum stopped when she spotted the tops of half a dozen heads behind a low wall. Then she crept towards it and peered over. Six lads leaped to their feet – one of them was Matt. In his hand was a cigarette. He flicked it to the floor as the other sinners scattered in all directions.

Mum gave Matt a lecture that lasted all the way

home. She told him he's not old enough to smoke and that it's a dirty, smelly habit and a waste of money. Matt wasn't bothered about any of that – his only worry was that one of us might tell Dad what he'd been up to.

We didn't tell him, but he found out anyway and Sunday dinner ended with a blazing row. It was the last meal the five of us ever had together.

We didn't eat our dinner until tea-time because Dad had been working. We had the usual – chicken with potatoes, peas and gravy, followed by our favourite, banana in custard. Barney gobbled up his custard so quickly that he kept making slurping noises. Dad gave him a dirty look.

'I can't help it,' said Barney. 'I've got a wobbly tooth, look.'

He waggled one of his front teeth with his tongue.

'You'll have a mouth full of wobbly teeth if you make that noise again,' said Dad.

Then Matt caused trouble. He said he had sixteen pieces of banana. I only had twelve.

'It's not fair,' I said. 'You always get loads more than me.'

'My pieces are really thick as well,' said Matt. 'Nearly as thick as you.'

I decided to measure mine, but when I picked a piece of banana out of the custard it slipped out of my hand on to the plastic tablecloth. It would have wiped off easily, but Dad went mad.

'Get up those stairs!'

'I didn't mean it.'

'Get up those stairs! It's like eating in Belle Vue zoo!'

Matt laughed and did an impression of a monkey. He bounced up and down with his hands curled under his armpits. Dad grabbed hold of Matt's sleeve and sniffed it.

'Have you been smoking?'

Matt stopped laughing.

'I'll ask you one more time. Have you been smoking?'

'No.'

'Own up now and I'll say no more about it.'

'It wasn't me, it was the lads from church.'

'If you tell me the truth that will be the end of it. Have you been smoking?'

Matt looked to Mum for help.

'Tell the truth, Matthew,' she said. 'Dad said that will be the end of the matter, if you tell the truth.'

'Yes,' Matt mumbled. 'But I only had a few puffs.'

Dad went crazy. He leaped to his feet, grabbed Matt by an ear and yelled into it.

'Get up those stairs you little liar! And if I see you again today I'll murder you!'

Then he turned on me. 'I've already told you! Stairs!' And Barney. 'You as well!'

'I haven't done anything,' said Barney.

'You've got manners like a pig.'

'But I – '

'Get up those stairs!'

'But – '

'Stairs!'

The three of us stomped out of the room. At the top of the stairs Barney yelled down to Dad.

'I'm going to live in a bungalow!'

We lay on our beds and played I-Spy. Me and Matt can't stand that game, but we didn't want Barney to start crying. We spent ages trying to guess something he'd spied beginning with S. It turned out to be ceiling.

After a while Mum came upstairs and gave us a biscuit for our supper. The last supper.

'Can we go back downstairs now?' asked Barney.

'No,' said Mum. 'Dad doesn't want to see you again today.'

'I didn't do anything!'

'You breathed didn't you?' said Matt. 'That's enough to make him hate you.'

'Dad doesn't hate you,' said Mum. 'He loves the three of you more than you'll ever know.'

'He's got a funny way of showing it,' said Matt.

Mum nodded. 'Yes, he has.' She sat on the edge of my bed. 'Dad's way of showing his love for you and for me is to work nearly every hour of the day. Do you know why he does that?'

We didn't answer.

'So he can earn enough money to buy food and clothes for us and so he can pay all the household bills. All that work makes him very tired and when he's tired he sometimes gets a bit short-tempered.'

'Sometimes?' said Matt. 'He's always in a foul mood. He's always having a go at us.'

'Dad should be drowned in the sea,' said Barney. 'That's what the vicar said. If somebody harms any of the children they should have a stone put round their neck and be drowned in the sea.'

Mum picked a few crumbs from my blanket. 'Perhaps we should try our best to be a bit more considerate,' she said.

I couldn't believe she was on his side.

'Perhaps we should bear in mind how tired he is and try not to wind him up so much. All that trouble at tea-time was caused by silly bickering about a banana, wasn't it?'

Mum stood up and closed the curtains.

'You might as well get ready for bed,' she said.

Me and Barney put our pyjamas on, but Matt

refused.

'I'm not going to bed at the same time as those two babies!'

Mum sighed. 'Please don't let's have any more bickering.'

She tucked me into bed and gave me a hug.

'Night, night, Samuel. I love you.'

I could smell her talcum powder – Lily of the Valley. Me and Matt and Barney bought it for her birthday out of our pocket money.

She gave Barney a hug.

'Night, night, Barnabas. I love you.'

She looked at Matt.

'Don't even think about it,' he said.

Mum was about to go downstairs when she gave us the news.

'You can all come to work with me tomorrow if you like.'

'Work?' I said. 'What work? What do you mean?'

'I've got a job. Mrs Bagshaw has asked me to work in the bread shop. You can be my assistants if you like.'

I could hardly believe it – with Mum working we'd be rich at last. We could go on holiday every month. For a fortnight. We'd live in a big house with a colour telly and a phone and an inside toilet. We'd have a huge garden so Mum could grow flowers. All we have at the moment is a patch of soil in the back yard next to the loo. Mum once planted some heather in it. (The soil, not the loo.) It died.

I hardly slept that night, I was so excited. I felt sure our lives were about to change. The very next day they did.

chapter 5

'We had a letter this morning, Samuel,' said Mum.
I stopped eating my cornflakes.

'From the hospital.'

I suddenly felt sick.

Mum took the letter out of the envelope that was on the sideboard. 'They want you to go in next week.'

Matt laughed. 'In the school holidays? Cruel.'

'I feel okay,' I said. 'I don't need to go to hospital. Tell them I don't need to go to hospital. Will you, Mum?'

Mum stroked my head. 'There's nothing to worry about, love. You'll only be in there for the day and then everything will be all right.'

'How do they take tonsils out?' asked Barney.

Matt grabbed the letter and had a look at it. 'It says here they use a carving knife.'

Mum told him to stop being silly. He took no notice and started reading.

'"A bed has been reserved for Samuel Bracegirdle under the care of Mr Silver."' Matt laughed. 'Mr Silver? He's a mad man, so I've heard.'

Mum told him off again. 'That's quite enough, Matthew.'

'Does it hurt?' asked Barney.

'No,' said Mum. 'Samuel won't feel a thing. The nurse will give him some special medicine to make him go to sleep and when he wakes up his tonsils will have gone.'

Mum took a carrier bag from the sideboard cupboard. She opened the bag and took out a purple dressing gown.

'I bought this for you, Samuel, to wear when you're in hospital. Do you want to try it on?'

I shook my head. 'I'm not going to hospital.'

'There's nothing to be frightened of, love. Come on, try on your dressing gown. If it's not the right size we can change it for another one.'

Mum slipped it over my clothes and fastened the cord around my waist.

'It's perfect,' she said. 'Do you like it?'

It was thick and warm and snug. I loved it, but I shrugged my shoulders as if I didn't know or care. I wish I hadn't done that – it must have cost a lot of money.

After breakfast, me, Barney and Mum went to work. Matt didn't want to go – he said he was too old to play 'shop'.

When somebody bought a loaf or a cake I took it out of the window and passed it to Barney. He was supposed to put it in a paper bag, but he wasn't very good at it so Mum gave him a hand.

At about ten o'clock Neville, Owen and Billy walked past the shop window just as I'd hoped they would. Their eyes nearly popped out of their heads when they saw me serving behind the counter. They sat on the pavement and watched until dinner-time.

'I think we did very well, don't you?' said Mum at the end of our shift. 'Here are your wages.'

She gave us both a lemon bun. Then she took her lifeboat charity box out of her shopping bag.

'I'm going collecting. Do you want to come with me?'

Barney said yes so I said no.

Mum turned the sign round on the door to show that the shop was 'closed' and we went outside. Neville and Owen and Billy were still there so I started to eat my lemon bun. They were really jealous.

'Will you do me a favour, Samuel?' asked Mum. 'Will you nip to Pendleton's for me? I need a box of washing powder.'

'Can I get the washing powder off the telly?' I said. 'We might win a holiday.'

'It's a bit expensive, love. Just get the cheapest.'

Owen smirked. He knew we couldn't afford the good stuff.

'We don't have to get the cheapest,' I said. 'Not any more. We can use your wages from your new job. How much money did you get paid today?'

'I didn't get paid any money, I did it as a favour for Mrs Bagshaw.'

'Tomorrow you should ask for a hundred pounds,' said Barney.

'I'm not working here tomorrow, love. It was just for this morning.'

I couldn't believe my ears. 'I thought you were working here every day,' I said.

'No. It was just while Mrs Bagshaw took her mother to the doctor's.'

Owen sniggered.

'That's no good!' I yelled. 'Who works for one morning? For no money! That's stupid!'

I threw my lemon bun on the ground and it splattered on the pavement.

'That's quite enough, Samuel,' said Mum.

'We're never going to be rich,' I said. 'We're never going to go on holiday. Tell her you want to work here every day.'

'She doesn't need somebody every – '

'Get a job at another shop then! What about Pendleton's? What about Mr Coffey at the grocers?'

'He's got Mrs Coffey to help him.'

'She's in a wheelchair, she's no good for anything!'

'Samuel – that's enough.'

Mum opened her purse and took out a few coins. 'Here's some money for the washing powder.'

'Go yourself!' I screamed. 'And why don't you collect some money for us instead of the stupid lifeboats, then we might not be so poor!'

Mum put the coins into her purse and, without looking, stepped off the pavement into the road. The car slammed into her. She was tossed into the air like a rag doll. Then she thumped down on to the bonnet. There was a screech of brakes and the car skidded and stopped. But Mum flew through the air, smacked head first into the road and rolled over three times. The charity box smashed on the ground in front of me. Dozens of coins ran around my feet.

chapter 6

'Come away from there.'
Somebody was tugging my sleeve.

'Come away.'

It was the woman that lives at number twenty. She took hold of Barney's hand.

'Come with me, boys.'

Loads of people were standing around – I don't know where they all came from.

'Come on, let's go to your Auntie Betty's.'

The driver of the car was sitting on the kerb, shaking.

'She just stepped out,' he kept saying. 'She just stepped out.'

Somebody was laying a coat over Mum to keep her warm.

'Come on, boys.'

Neville was on his hands and knees snapping up the pennies that should have gone to the lifeboatmen.

'Come on!'

As soon as Auntie Betty opened her front door she seemed to know something was wrong.

'What's happened?'

The woman from number twenty took a deep breath. 'Betty, there's been an accident. It's Hannah. She's been knocked down. Outside Bagshaw's shop.'

Auntie Betty ran down the pavement in her slippers. Me and Barney were ready to run after her, but the woman from number twenty pushed us into the house as if she owned the place.

'Stop here,' she said.

She couldn't stand still. She kept going up and down the lobby and looking out of the front door. After a while, Mrs Pendleton turned up. The two of them whispered on the doorstep. They were desperate to let Dad know what had happened. They knew where he worked, but didn't have a phone number. In the end Mrs Pendleton decided to try and find the vicar. I don't know why because he wouldn't have had a clue what the number was.

'I want to go home,' said Barney.

The woman from number twenty grabbed a piece of paper and a pencil off the sideboard.

'Why don't you boys have a game of Noughts and Crosses?'

We played about five hundred games. I wasn't really thinking and Barney beat me for the first time ever.

It was well past tea-time before we were allowed to go home. Dad was there with Auntie Betty, Matt and Donald Duck. He was wearing his vicar's collar even though it wasn't Sunday and had his serious face on.

'Where's Mum?' asked Barney.

Donald sat on the settee and told me and Barney to sit next to him.

'Today, boys, God decided to try and find a new helper,' he said. 'He wanted to choose the most special person he could find in the whole world and he could think of nobody more special than your mummy.'

He looked at me and Barney as if we were supposed to say something, but we didn't so he carried on.

'So your mummy is now on her way to be a special helper in heaven. Do you understand, boys?'

'Is it like being one of Father Christmas's helpers?' asked Barney.

'Yes, it's a bit like that Barnabas,' said Donald with a big nod of his head. 'But instead of helping Father Christmas, mummy is going to be helping God.'

'Will she be back for tea?'

'No. No, mummy won't be back for tea. In fact, your mummy is so special that God wants her to stay in heaven for ever.'

Donald stood up and patted me and Barney on our heads. He nodded to Dad and left.

Dad rubbed his hands slowly all over his face as if he was having a wash without any water. He looked at me and Matt and Barney. We looked at Auntie Betty. She looked as if she wanted to cry, but was desperately trying not to. None of us spoke. It was as if the five of us were playing a game – next one to speak loses. Eventually Barney cracked.

'I'm hungry.'

'Would you like some chips?' asked Auntie Betty.

'Mum said we could have bangers and mash.'

'We'll have that another time. I'll go and get some chips.'

She left the four of us to have another go at the silence game.

After what seemed like an hour Auntie Betty returned with three vinegar-soaked parcels. She handed them to me, Matt and Barney and then went into the kitchen with Dad. I thought they'd gone to get the plates, but they shut the door and tried to whisper to each other. Auntie Betty wasn't very good at it.

'I'm not here for your benefit, Jack Bracegirdle ... those three sweet little lambs in there ... it's my sister we're talking about ...'

Barney asked Matt if they were having an argument.

'Yes,' he said. 'But at least they're talking. It's the first time they've spoken to each other in over a year.'

Auntie Betty burst out of the kitchen and stormed to the front door.

'I'll see you in the morning, boys.'

Dad chased after her and shoved something into her hand.

'Here,' he grunted.

'What's this?'

'Money for the chips.'

Auntie Betty looked at him and shook her head. 'God help you, Jack.'

The front door slammed.

'What's for pudding?' said Barney.

Dad didn't answer and Barney knew not to ask again.

For a while the four of us sat staring at the television. Eventually Barney asked Dad if he could switch it on. Dad nodded – I think he was glad of something to break the silence.

We gawped at the TV for the rest of the evening. 'Dad's Army' was on. We'd seen that episode before so none of us laughed. The people in the audience thought it was hilarious, they were shrieking with laughter and I wanted to tell them to shut up. Slowly it went dark around us, but we didn't bother to turn on the light. The telly made big shadows on the wall and lit up our faces. In the flickering glow Dad's skin was a strange grey colour, his cheeks were hollow and each line was now a deep crack. He looked just like an old man.

'Go on up to bed,' he said, without taking his eyes off the screen.

Me and Barney trudged up the stairs. I switched on the bedroom light and closed the curtains. We put on our pyjamas, climbed into our beds and waited. I guess we were waiting for Mum to come and tuck us in, give us a hug and tell us she loves us as she had done every night of our lives.

'I want the curtain cars,' mumbled Barney.

I turned off the light and opened the curtains ever so slightly. A car came down the lane and its headlights shone through the tiny gap in the curtains and flickered all around the bedroom walls before vanishing. It was followed by another and another. The dancing lights usually sent us to sleep, but for the first time ever they had no effect.

We were still awake when Matt came into the bedroom. He flopped on to his bed and lay on his back in the dark.

'Will Mum be back tomorrow, Matt?' said Barney.

Matt didn't say anything.

'Matt, will Mum be back tomorrow?'

'No. It's like the vicar said. She's never coming back.'

'It's Sam's fault.'

'What do you mean?'

'Mum asked him to go to the shop and he said no, so she had to go herself and that's when she got knocked down.'

Matt sat up quickly. 'Is that true?'

I didn't answer.

He pounced on top of me. I scrambled under the covers, but it didn't make any difference – I still felt every thump.

'You killed her! Do (thump) you (thump) un- (thump) der- (thump) stand? You killed her!'

chapter 7

I woke with a shiver. My pyjamas felt cold. Cold and damp. I realised what I'd done. But I hadn't wet the bed in years! I leaped out of bed and quickly pulled the stained sheet off the mattress. Barney and Matt were watching. I expected them to laugh or tease, but they just stared at me as if I was a dirty animal.

I slouched down the stairs with the sheet trailing behind me. Dad was sitting in the living room – I think he'd been there all night. He hadn't had a shave and he looked like Desperate Dan. When he saw the sheet he jumped from his chair and dragged me into the kitchen. He made me take off my wet pyjamas and stuff them into the washing machine with the bedding.

He whipped open a cupboard door. 'Where's the washing powder?' He slammed it shut again. He worked his way round the kitchen, opening and slamming.

'Where the hell does she keep it?'

'We haven't got any,' I said quietly.

Dad sent me upstairs to get dressed. When I went back down he held out a handful of coins.

'Go to the shop and buy some.'

'No.'

I'd have to cross the road where it had happened. The exact same place.

'Do it!'

'I'm not going.'

Dad raised his arm as a warning and I took the money.

Outside the bread shop I stood on the kerb and did the road safety drill Mum had drummed in to me years before. Look right, look left, look right again.

'If there are any cars coming, Samuel, wait until they've gone and start again.'

Look right, look left, look right again.

'It doesn't matter if you have to wait all day, don't cross until it's safe.'

I looked right, left and right again. Then I looked down. There was a blood stain on the road.

I ran across with tears streaming down my face. Pendleton's wasn't open so I sat on the step and waited. Opposite, Mrs Bagshaw was putting loaves in the bread shop window. When she saw me she came over.

'What are you doing sitting here, Samuel?'

I wiped my eyes. 'Waiting to buy some washing powder.'

'What do you want washing powder for?'

'To wash with.'

'It's only seven o'clock. Does your daddy know you're here?'

'It's him that's going to do the washing.'

I sat there for ages. Every time Mrs Baghsaw put something in her window she looked over and gave me a sad smile.

It's your fault, I thought. If you hadn't taken your stupid mum to the doctor's it wouldn't have happened. It's your mum's fault for being ill. It's the doctor's fault.

At last Mrs Pendleton arrived. 'Hello, Samuel. What are you doing sitting here?'

'Waiting to buy some washing powder. To wash with.'

She opened the door and the smells of the shop wafted out on to the street – paraffin, bleach and the sawdust that's sprinkled over the wooden floor. I followed her inside where she reached up to a shelf and took down a box of washing powder.

Big red letters screamed out from the side of the box: 'Buy me for your chance to win a family holiday!'

'I don't want that one,' I said. 'I want the cheapest.'

She exchanged it for another box and I slapped the money on the counter. She counted it out and gave me back a few of the coins.

When I got home Auntie Betty was there. She gave us all our breakfast and then washed the dishes. She washed the sheet and my pyjamas and made the beds.

Dad didn't go to work. He spent all morning answering the front door and talking to people on the doorstep. We'd never had so many visitors – people from church and people off our street. I don't think Dad knew who half of them were.

'If there's anything we can do,' they said.

What could *they* do?

'I'm so sorry.'

What were *they* sorry for? It's wasn't *their* fault she was dead.

Donald Duck came round again. Me and Barney had to leave the room while he had a chat with Dad and Auntie Betty. Matt was allowed to stay as if he'd suddenly become one of the grown-ups. Perhaps he had. I sat on the stairs and tried to hear what they were saying.

Donald did all the talking. 'I've spoken to Mr Greaves about the funeral ... the morgue ... hard to understand ... just the beginning ... a better place ... '

When the vicar left, Dad went with him. As soon as they'd gone Matt told Auntie Betty he was going out as well.

'Where are you going Matthew?'

'Dunno, but I'm not stopping here with a babysitter.'

He stormed off.

'Where's Dad gone with the vicar?' asked Barney.

'They have things to do,' said Auntie Betty.

'The funeral,' I said.

'What's the funeral?' asked Barney. 'Auntie Betty, what's the funeral?'

'What's the morgue?' I asked.

'Let's have a game of Snakes and Ladders,' suggested Auntie Betty.

Barney cheated. He thought I hadn't seen him, but I let him get away with it. Auntie Betty didn't notice. She was staring at the board as if she'd been hypnotised. We had to keep telling her when it was her turn to roll the dice. One game followed another and the afternoon lasted for ever.

Matt came home when he was hungry and Auntie Betty made us bangers and mash. She didn't have anything to eat, but she sat at the table with us while we had ours. I could tell she was desperately trying to think of things to say. It was as if she wanted to start a conversation before we asked any awkward questions.

'Is bangers and mash your favourite, Barnabas?'

Barney nodded.

'What about you, Sam?'

I shrugged my shoulders.

'Matthew?'

Nothing.

'And what's your favourite television programme, Barnabas?'

'Captain Pugwash. I've got the same name as one of the sailors on his ship.'

'And what are your favourite sweets?'

'Pink shrimps.'

'I'll see if I can bring you a pink shrimp tomorrow.'

'Are you going to come every day?' asked Barney. 'Are you going to live here?'

'No, no. I'm just helping out.'

'Are you going to mend my socks?'

'Do they need mending?'

Barney got down from the table and fished his socks out of the sewing basket in the corner of the room.

'If they don't get mended I'll have to give them to the vicar.'

'Why?' asked Auntie Betty.

'Because they're holy!'

I don't know if Barney fully understood that Mum was never coming back. I understood it, but when I heard the back door open I still thought it was her. Just for a second. She'd popped to the shops, that's all. She'd been to visit somebody who was ill or out with one of her collecting boxes, but she was back now.

Auntie Betty took our plates into the kitchen and within minutes Dad was arguing with her again. She didn't bother trying to whisper this time.

'They're too young!' she shouted. 'It's just not done!'

'If I say they're going, they're going!'

'What are you trying to prove? Poor lambs won't have any idea what's going on. Or are you going to explain it to them? Because I'm not.'

Barney asked Matt what they were rowing about.

'Dad wants us all to go to the funeral.'

'What's the funeral?'

'You'll see.'

chapter 8

That night my dreams were crazy and horrible, but at last the sound of clinking bottles woke me up. It was the milkman. It was morning and my bed was dry!

Auntie Betty didn't come which made the day seem even longer.

'Who's going to make our breakfast?' asked Barney.

'You're going to have to learn to do things for yourself from now on,' said Dad.

He gave us all jobs. He told Barney to set the table for every meal, Matt to wash the dishes and me to dry them. When Barney was setting the table for breakfast he put too many bowls out. He put one out for Mum. We all stared at it as we ate our cornflakes.

It felt strange having breakfast with Dad. He was usually at work by the time we got up. It was weird having him in the house during the day. It didn't feel right. He was in the way and I couldn't wait for him to go out.

'Make sure these bowls are washed and put away by the time I get back,' he said.

'Where are you going?' asked Barney.

'To see the vicar to sort things out.'

'When are you going to work?'

'When things get back to normal.'

As soon as Dad had gone, Matt leaned across the table and slapped me across the head. 'Things will never get back to normal because of you!'

I told him to get lost and he gave me another slap.

'Wash the bowls!' he snarled.

'That's your job. I'm supposed to dry them.'

'You're going to wash *and* dry. Got it?'

'Naff off.'

He leaped to his feet, charged into me and knocked me off my chair. He dived on top of me and pinned my shoulders to the floor with his knees like a wrestler on the telly.

'From now on, you're going to do everything because it's all *your* fault!'

I tried to get free, but it was hopeless. The more I moved the more he pressed down with his knees. It was agony.

Then I began to cry and he let me go. I ran upstairs, lay on my bed and imagined what I was going to do to him in years to come. When I'm older I'll be as big as him. One day, when he's not expecting it, I'll tap him on the shoulder. When he turns round I'll knock his teeth right down his throat.

I stayed in the bedroom nearly all day. Every so often Barney knocked on the door. He couldn't get in because I'd shoved my bed against it. He sat outside on the stairs.

'It wasn't really your fault, Sam.'

'Leave me alone.'

I didn't go downstairs until I heard Dad come back. Matt had washed the bowls. Dad gave me a clip round the ear and told me to dry them.

He made beans on burned toast. As we ate he gave me and Matt and Barney our instructions for the following day.

'I want you three ready for quarter past ten,' he said. 'The funeral car is coming at half past.'

'Wow!' said Barney. 'We're going in a car?'

'Make sure you've all had a proper wash.'

Barney was more interested in the transport. 'What sort of car?'

'A black one. Wear the clothes you would wear for Sunday school.'

'Who's going to drive it?'

'The driver.'

'Can I sit next to the driver?'

'Are you listening to me? What time do you have to be ready?'

'Half past ten?'

'Quarter past!'

'And we have to wear our Sunday school clothes,' said Barney. 'But it's Thursday tomorrow so that makes them Thursday school clothes, but school is shut for the holidays so we can't wear anything. We'll be in the nude.'

'Any messing about from you tomorrow and you'll be sorry you were ever born.'

After tea Dad made us all fetch our shoes from the pantry. I thought he was going to make us clean them, but he offered to do it for us. Dad loves cleaning shoes. I once asked him why.

'You can tell a lot about a person by their shoes,' he said.

He spread some newspaper over the carpet and laid out his kit – a tin of black polish, a tin of brown polish (which he hardly ever uses), two brushes and a duster. Then he rolled up his shirt sleeves and slipped one of his own shoes over his left hand. With the other hand he dabbed a brush into the tin of black polish and set to work. With slow even movements he gently worked the polish into the surface of the shoe, all the time moving it around on his hand as if it was a glove puppet.

When he was satisfied that the shoe was covered evenly with the black stuff he placed it on the newspaper and moved on to shoe number two. When all eight had been treated he returned to the first one and with short sharp strokes of the second brush he began to polish. Every so often he would stop and hold the shoe up to his face as if it was a mirror – he wasn't satisfied until he could see his reflection in the brilliant blackness. Occasionally he'd spot a tiny blemish and would spit on it and work in the saliva with his duster. Then he'd add a bit more polish before giving the shoe another buffing. Finally he wiped the sweat from his brow with the back of his hand, sat back in his chair and admired his handiwork. The four pairs of shoes were as good as new and wouldn't have looked out of place in a shop window.

Dad spent the evening in his bedroom. After a while I went up to see what he was doing. I stood by the door and watched as he stuffed all of Mum's shoes into her shopping bag. Her coats and dresses were piled up on the bed.

'What are you doing?' I asked.

'Having a sort out.'

He picked up some items from the dressing table and dropped them into a carrier bag – Mum's hairbrush with some of her hairs tangled in it, a tin of Nivea cream, a box of tissues. He didn't know what to do with Mum's Bible.

'Do you want this?'

'No.'

It went in the bag with everything else. A tin of talcum powder was about to follow. It was the one that me and Matt and Barney had bought.

'I'll have that,' I said.

I held it to my nose. Lily of the Valley. For a second Mum was there.

Dad tied the handles of the carrier bag in a knot, dropped it on the floor and clapped his hands together. Job done.

'We'll show 'em, won't we, son?' he said.

'Show who?'

'Everybody.'

'Show 'em what?'

'That we can cope.'

chapter 9

'They're here.'

Matt was peeping out through the curtains. We weren't allowed to open them, we had to leave them closed all day because that's what you do when somebody dies. Me and Barney rushed to the window to have a look at the two big black cars pulling up outside our house. One of them had a coffin in the back and it made me think of a joke I'd heard at school. A man was driving a funeral car up a steep hill. The coffin slid out of the back and rolled away so the driver stopped outside a chemist. He ran inside and said 'Have you got anything to stop my coffin?' I knew I shouldn't be thinking about it, but I couldn't help it.

Barney asked Matt if the cars were Rolls Royces. Matt said the one with the coffin in it was a Bentley and the other was a limousine.

'Come away from that window!'

Dad was rapidly tying his tie in front of the mirror. After all his warnings about being ready he was the one running late. One of his shoelaces had snapped and he'd turned the house upside down looking for another.

There was a knock on the front door and Dad tried to look calm as he answered it. It was the men from the Bentley. They began to carry all the flowers out to the car. There were mountains of them in the lobby – people had been arriving with them all morning.

Dad put his jacket on. He looked really uncomfortable – as if he was wearing somebody else's clothes.

'Come here so that I can look at you,' he said.

He made us line up like soldiers for inspection. He clicked his fingers and pointed at Barney's socks which needed pulling up. Another click for me to straighten my tie and one for Matt to comb his hair.

'Your mother would be proud of you,' he said.

Barney burst into tears. Dad took a handkerchief from his pocket and offered it to him, but he wouldn't take it. He just stood there blubbering. I put my hand on his shoulder.

'It's okay, Barney,' I said.

He shrugged me away and pointed at the sideboard. Coconut was floating on top of the water in the fruit bowl. Dead.

'Wipe your eyes and go and get in the car,' said Dad, shoving his hanky into Barney's hand. He picked up the fruit bowl and headed for the kitchen.

'What are you going to do with Coconut?' I asked. 'Where are you – '

'Get in the car.'

Outside, Neville and Owen and Billy were skulking around the limousine and Billy's mum had to drag them away. The driver opened the door for us, we climbed inside and sat in a row on a long springy seat. After a few minutes Dad joined us.

Some of the neighbours were standing on their doorsteps – they'd probably never seen a limo before and the driver pulled away really slowly so that everybody could have a good look.

Donald Duck met us at the church door. He had a quick word with Dad and then organised us into a line.

Donald was at the front followed by the funeral men carrying the coffin. Then Dad, Matt, me and Barney.

The organ played a dreary tune as we made our way up the aisle. I'd never seen so many people in church. We were surrounded on either side by hundreds of black hats, black dresses, black coats and black suits. We walked between them like judges at the World Dandruff Championship.

For a moment I thought there were no empty seats, but Auntie Betty had saved us some on the front row.

After a few hymns and prayers Donald made a speech about Mum. He said she always put everybody else before herself, she always went out of her way to help others and always did so with a smile on her face. He said it was hard to understand why such a faithful servant had been taken away and some of us might be feeling a bit angry about it. We might even be looking for somebody to blame.

Matt dug his elbow in my ribs. 'You!' he whispered.

I tried to thump him, but he grabbed my wrist and slowly twisted my arm. He was killing me, but I couldn't shout out because Donald was still talking and you could have heard a pin drop.

'At this time it is important to treasure the many happy memories we have of Hannah ...'

Matt kicked my ankle.

'Indeed we should give thanks. Thanks for the way she enriched all our lives.'

He was pinching the skin on my arm and wouldn't let go. I wanted to scream.

'Let us give thanks for the fact that Hannah lives on through her three fine boys of whom she was very proud.'

Everybody was looking at us. Matt released me.

The service ended with Mum's favourite hymn:

'What a friend we have in Jesus,
All our sins and grief to bear.'

Some of the adults in the choir didn't sing because they were crying. That set a load of others off. Dad didn't cry, but I reckon he should have made the effort. I tried, but nothing would come out. Perhaps he was the same.

Suddenly Matt burst into tears. He was squawking like a two-year-old. But Barney sang the hymn as if nothing had happened.

On the way out of church I spotted a group of women standing at the back. They must have turned up late. They weren't regulars and they looked a bit out of sorts – as if they didn't belong. I knew I'd seen two of them somewhere before and I tried to think where it was. Then I remembered. St Mary's Fayre. One of them was the woman that had been so pleased to see Mum and the other was the one that Barney had nearly killed with a dart. Catholics were in our church. Mum's bridge had been built.

Outside, people patted Dad on the back and shook his hand as if he'd done something marvellous. A man offered him a cigarette. Dad said no, but then changed his mind and took it. I'd never seen him smoke before and he looked odd.

We got back into our limo and were driven to a graveyard. We stood round a hole as the coffin was lowered into it. When it was in the ground Dad and Auntie Betty threw bits of soil onto it.

Barney tugged on Auntie Betty's coat. 'What's in that box?'

'Flowers.'

We went to Auntie Betty's for a party which seemed a strange thing to do – we never had a party there when Mum was alive. There was luncheon meat and corned beef as well as Cheddar and Cheshire cheese. There was a jar of mixed pickles and a choice of white or brown bread. For afters there were Jaffa Cakes (Barney had four, I had three) and Penguins (two each). Loads of people from church were there. Some of the women drank sherry and some of the men had shandy. (Somebody left some in a glass and Matt drank it when nobody was looking.)

There was loads of grub left at the end and Auntie Betty gave it to us to take home for our supper. We ate it while we watched the telly.

'My tummy feels funny,' said Barney.

'Serves you right for stuffing your face,' said Dad.

'I feel sick.'

'Get to the toilet. I don't want you chucking up in here.'

'It's dark,' said Barney feebly. 'Mum takes us when it's dark. She holds the torch.'

'Mum's not here, is she?'

'Will you come with me, Sam?'

'No.'

'Go with him,' said Dad.

'Why should I?'

'Because I said so, that's why.'

I got the torch from the kitchen cupboard and we set off down the yard. I whirled the beam around in the sky as if it was a searchlight in a war film.

'Shine it on the path!' said Barney.

He was worried there might be spiders crawling around his feet in the dark and made me shine the torch all around the white stone walls of the loo before he would go inside.

'What's that?' he whispered.

'It's only a cobweb. Cobwebs can't hurt you.'

Barney knelt down on the stone floor and gripped

the sides of the toilet bowl. Suddenly he leaped to his feet and let out an ear-piercing scream. His whole body was shaking.

'What is it?' I said.

Barney was staring into the toilet. Staring back with one eye was Coconut. He was floating on his side on top of the water. I quickly reached for the chain to flush him away.

'No!' screamed Barney.

'We can't leave him here.'

Before Barney could argue I gave a yank on the chain. Coconut spun round and round in the ferocious whirlpool, but he wouldn't go away. Barney began to cry. I pulled a few sheets of toilet paper off the roll and held them in one hand. Then I closed my eyes and put my other hand into the freezing water and fished around until I had hold of Coconut. He was hard and slippery. I slapped him on to the crisp, dry paper and wrapped him up. Then I carefully carried him down the yard to Mum's little garden. Barney held the torch while I crouched down and dug a hole in the ground and placed Coconut in it. Then me and Barney threw little bits of soil on top of his body before covering him up completely.

chapter 10

With everything that had happened I hoped Dad would forget about my operation. Either that or he'd ask them to cancel it. No chance.

Two days later I followed him along miles of hospital corridor which stank of disinfectant. He kept asking people where we should go. Finally, a man pointed us through a pair of big swing doors into a long ward with beds down each side. In every bed, but one, was a child. Sitting next to every bed, but one, was a mum.

Dad handed the letter to a nurse. 'Are we in the right place?'

'You certainly are.'

The nurse patted the empty bed. 'Do you want to put your pyjamas on, Samuel, and jump in here?'

'I'm not tired.'

She smiled and pulled a curtain round the bed. I put my pyjamas on reluctantly and slid between the stiff sheets while Dad put my clothes and things in the small bedside cabinet.

'I'll see you later,' he mumbled.

He pulled back the curtain and left.

All around the ward mums were hugging and kissing their children. Tall mums, short mums, thin mums and fat mums. Eventually they managed to tear themselves away and walk to the end of the ward. When they reached the doors each one gave a big wave and blew a final kiss to their child before leaving, some of them with tears in their eyes.

I wondered if ladies had to go to a special place to learn how to be a mum; 'Mum School'. Term would start with household chores – how to bake, cook, sew, clean and iron. Then how to deal with all the yucky stuff – pooh, puke and piddle. On to bedtime duties – tucking your child into bed, hugging them so tight it makes them feel safe, letting them get into your bed in the middle of the night if they're having a bad dream. And, finally, the toughest test of all – the one that sorts out the *real* mums – how to spit on a handkerchief in a lady-like way so you can wipe a dirty mark off your child's face.

At the end of term they'd give an award to The Mum of the Year.

'And once again the winner is … Hannah Bracegirdle!'

All the other mums would smile and clap. They wouldn't be jealous. They'd agree that Mum was the best at everything and wish they could be like her.

'Sadly Hannah can't be here to collect the award because her son wouldn't go for a box of washing powder.'

I climbed down from the bed, opened the bedside cabinet and took out my dressing gown. When I slipped it on it felt as if Mum was wrapping her arms around me and giving me a big hug. I began to cry.

'I'm sorry, Mum.'

I couldn't stop.

'I'm sorry … I'm sorry.'

All the other kids were looking at me, so I lay on the bed and sobbed into the pillow.

In my head I could see all the people crying in church. I could hear them all choking on the words of Mum's favourite hymn.

'What a friend we have in Jesus,
All our sins and grief to bear.
What a privilege to carry
Everything to God in prayer.'

Miss Wilmslow once told us that God is always listening out for our prayers. If we want something we only have to ask and he will give it to us. I'd tried it a few times, but I'd never had any results.

Last Christmas Owen got a bike. He thought he was really something riding up and down our street so I asked God to make him fall off, but he didn't do it. When Miss Stern said she was going to choose somebody from our class to play the cymbals in the school orchestra I prayed every night for a week, but I didn't get the job. When the doctor said he was going to send a letter about my operation I begged for it to go to the wrong address and never be seen again. God ignored me as usual.

'O what peace we often forfeit,
O what needless pain we bear.
All because we do not carry
Everything to God in prayer.'

I decided to give it one last go.

'Dear God, please let me see my mum again so I can tell her I'm sorry. Do this or I'll never speak to you again. Amen.'

'Would you like a nice book to read?'

An old lady was standing by the bed. She had a set of shelves on wheels. A poster was stuck on the end of it: 'Children's library sponsored by The Mothers' Union.'

'I've got *The Famous Five* or *The Secret Seven* or how about *The Boys' Book of Rockets*?'

I wiped my eyes and shook my head.

'Shall I choose one for you?' She took a book from the top shelf and placed it on the end of the bed. 'There you are.'

She pushed her way from one bed to another. Nobody wanted a book, but she gave them one anyway.

'Here we are, Samuel. A nice drink for you.'

A nurse handed me a tiny glass container full of red liquid. I knew what it was – the special medicine to make me go to sleep. It didn't taste too bad.

I watched her go round the ward giving everybody the magic potion. Some of the kids were already asleep and the nurse woke them up to give it to them which seemed a bit daft.

After about twenty minutes I was the only one that hadn't nodded off. What would happen if the medicine had no effect on me? Would they do the operation while I was awake?

I closed my eyes, but I couldn't get to sleep. I tried counting sheep jumping over a fence, but gave up after about six hundred. Then I remembered something I'd heard on 'The Comedians'. One of them said when he can't get to sleep he always lies on the edge of his bed. He soon drops off. I didn't fancy trying it – this bed was too high.

I reached for the book at the end of the bed. Whenever Miss Wilmslow read a story at Sunday school half of the kids fell asleep, so it was worth a go.

On the front cover was a picture of a man drowning in the sea. His head was just above the water. He looked a bit like Dad when he was younger – Dad the sailor that I'd seen in that old photograph. This man wasn't smiling though – he looked absolutely terrified. He was desperately stretching out a hand towards another hand that was reaching into the picture. Underneath, the title of the book was in big gold letters: *Nothing Is Impossible*.

The first page showed a ship smashing into some rocks:

'Douglas Bay, Isle of Man. 1820. Many ships were wrecked. Many lives were lost.'

The next picture was a crowd of people watching the sailors drown:

'Nobody did anything to help.'

A picture of an old man wearing a three-cornered hat speaking to the crowd:

'Until somebody stepped forward. His name was William Hillary.'

A picture of Hillary and twelve young men in a big rowing boat:

'With the help of volunteers, Hillary staged many rescues and saved many lives.'

A hand ripped the book from my grasp.

'You're supposed to be asleep!'

A man with long greasy hair and a green coat flung the book on to the cabinet and started fiddling with the legs on my bed.

'I'm glad I'm not you,' he said. 'Going for an operation with Mr Silver. He can't see properly. He should wear glasses. Last time he cut out a kid's tongue by mistake.'

My bed began to move. It was on wheels. The man was behind me, pushing me towards the doors at the end of the ward.

'Mr Silver used to be a butcher, you know. He's got a set of extra sharp knives for slicing open little boys.'

We crashed through the doors.

'And he's got a big meat cleaver for chopping off hands and feet.'

We sped along the corridor.

'And if you survive this operation, there's worse to come. He'll follow you everywhere you go. One night he'll be hiding in your bedroom waiting to hack off an arm or a leg.'

Bang! Through more doors into a darkened room. As the doors closed behind me it became even darker. My bed stopped moving. I couldn't see anybody, but I knew there were people standing all around me.

'Hello, Samuel,' said a voice in the blackness. 'I'm Mr Silver.'

I didn't answer.

'Do you see those balloons over there, Samuel?'

I couldn't see any balloons. I couldn't see anything.

'I want you to help me blow them up. Will you do that? Will you help me?'

'I can't see them,' I said quietly.

'That's because they're black balloons and it's very dark in here. I'll just put this special mask on your face and it will help you to blow them up.'

A strong rubbery stench filled my nostrils. He was going to gas me.

'Big breaths,' said Mr Silver.

'I can't ... see them.'

'Don't worry about that, just blow them up.'

'I ... can't ... see ... '

I reached out my hand, but Mum wasn't there to hold it.

chapter 11

'Are you alive or what?'
I could hear Dad's voice.

'Wake up, you dopey lump.'

I forced my eyes open. I was back in the ward. Dad was sitting next to the bed. I sat up as quickly as I could and was relieved to find all my limbs were still attached. I looked around. A few of the kids looked as if they were dead. One lad was mumbling in his sleep. Some mums were sitting next to their children gently stroking their hands just as they'd been taught at Mum School.

I swallowed and my throat felt sore so I tried not to do it again.

'Have ... ' My voice was croaky. 'Have ... they ...?'

Dad nodded. 'All done.'

More mums arrived. They rushed to their child's bedside and smothered them with kisses.

'I've got something to tell you when we get home,' said Dad.

I could tell by the way he said it that he thought it was good news. He probably wanted me to beg him to tell me there and then, but I couldn't be bothered.

After a while a nurse took my temperature. She said it was fine and I could go home.

Matt and Barney were lying on the floor watching the telly. Barney leaped to his feet.

'What was it like, Sam? Was it worse than the dentist?'

I nodded.

'Was it worse than having to eat liver every day?'

I nodded again.

'Could you feel them cutting your throat?' asked Matt. 'Shame they didn't make a better job of it.'

Dad took off his coat and hung it up rather than flinging it at Matt as usual. Then he helped me off with my coat and hung that up too. He was being nice. Something was going on. He asked Matt to turn the telly down.

'We're watching it.'

'Turn it down for a minute, please. Now that we're all here I've got something to say. It's a surprise.'

'What sort of surprise?' asked Barney.

'Turn the telly down and I'll tell you.'

'Tell us while we're watching it,' said Matt.

Dad switched it off.

'The surprise is this,' he said with a big smile. 'We're all going on holiday!'

We looked at him as if he was speaking a foreign language.

'Holiday?' said Matt. 'When?'

'Saturday.'

'Where?'

'The Isle of Man.'

'Never heard of it.'

'It's an island.'

'In Ireland?' said Barney.

'No, an island. In between England and Ireland and Scotland and Wales.'

'Can we go to Blackpool instead?'

'No.'

'Can we go to Benidorm?' said Matt. 'A lad at school has been there. He went on an aeroplane!'

'Bully for him,' said Dad. 'We're going to the Isle of Man and that's the end of it.'

Dad's smile had disappeared as quickly as it had arrived. He looked to me for some enthusiasm.

'What have you got to say for yourself? You've always wanted to go on holiday.'

'That was before,' I mumbled.

'If you don't want to come you can stop at home on your own.'

'Can I stop at home on my own?' said Matt.

'You can all stop at home as far as I'm concerned,' said Dad. 'Do you want to go or shall I cancel it?'

'What's at this place?' asked Barney.

'I don't know, I've never been.'

'Is it the seaside?'

'Of course it is, it's an island.'

'Is there a funfair?' asked Matt. 'I'll go if there's a funfair. How long are we going for?'

'Three nights.'

'That's not a proper holiday,' I said.

'I thought you were stopping at home on your own,' said Dad.

'I am. I'm just saying that's not a proper holiday. A proper holiday is a week.'

'Well this holiday is three nights.'

'I'm definitely not going then.'

Dad leaned into my face. 'Don't be so awkward. You're going and you'll like it!'

'I'm not and I won't!'

There was a knock on the front door. Dad clicked his fingers and sent Matt to answer it. Matt came back with a plate piled high with jam doughnuts.

'Mrs Bagshaw sent these!'

Dad took the plate from Matt. 'If we want cakes, we'll buy them.'

He went into the kitchen. We followed and watched him drop the doughnuts one by one into the bin.

'We're not a ruddy charity!'

chapter 12

The nurse had warned me I might feel a bit tired for a day or two and she was right. When I woke up Barney and Matt were already dressed and gone. I put my clothes on and wandered downstairs. I could hear Donald Duck talking to Dad and Matt in the living room. I couldn't be bothered trying to listen in. I went outside.

Neville and Owen and Billy were sitting on the pavement near Owen's house. I was going to tell them about my operation, but Barney was filling them in about the holiday.

'It's the seaside.'

'So what?' said Owen.

'And it's an island.'

'Big deal.'

I told Barney to put a sock in it, but he just kept going on and on.

'We're going to go on the beach and we're going to go on the funfair and – '

'We know why you're going,' said Owen. 'We know how you can afford it all of a sudden.'

I asked him what he was on about.

'I've just seen Donald Duck going in your house.'

'So?'

'I bet he's dropping off the money.'

'What money?'

'For your holiday.'

'What are you talking about?'

'Don't you get it? The church is paying for your holiday.'

'Are they hell!'

'They had a collection. They always do for dead people. Especially dead poor people.'

I told him to shut his mouth.

'Make me. They had a meeting at church and Donald said he felt really sorry for you because you've never been on holiday and your dad's only a warehouseman and your mum never had a job in her life.'

'Shut it!'

I jumped on top of him and tried to thump him, but he grabbed my arm and punched me in the face. I got to my feet and wiped my nose with the back of my hand to see if it was bleeding. It was. I began to walk home. Barney followed. Suddenly he stopped and yelled at Owen.

'Mum did have a job! She worked in the bread shop!'

'Yeah, for one morning!' shouted Owen. 'And she didn't even get any dough!'

He started singing 'Where's your mamma gone? Where's-your-*mamma*-gone? Far, far away!'

He tried to get Billy and Neville to join in, but they wouldn't. Instead they got to their feet and went home.

Dad and Matt were sipping tea with Donald Duck as if they were best buddies. The mood soon changed when me and Barney burst in on their cosy chat.

Dad spotted the blood on my shirt. 'What the hell have you been doing?'

'Owen smacked him on the nose,' said Barney.

Matt laughed. 'Crusty bogeys for supper.'

I marched up to Donald. 'Are you paying for our holiday?'

He laughed nervously. 'Not personally, no.' He laughed again, but stopped when he realised nobody else was joining in.

'Is church paying?' I said.

He put on his serious face. 'It's like this, Samuel. At St Peter's we have what's known as a fellowship fund and it's used for all sorts of things. In fact your mummy often helped me to organise it. She was a great organiser your mummy. And yes, sometimes, it's used for people to have a little holiday.'

'We're not a ruddy charity.'

Dad shot forward in his chair. 'Watch your mouth!'

Donald continued quickly. 'You see, Samuel, we have a special arrangement with St George's in Douglas, that's a place on the Isle of Man. The vicar there is a very good friend of mine. And I thought, and some of our commit-tee thought, that you and Matthew and Barnabas and your daddy might like – '

'I don't want to go.'

'That's what your daddy said at first. But I told him that your mummy spent lots of her time asking others to give. Indeed there are times when it's good to give, but there are also times when it's good to take.'

'I'm not going.'

Donald put on an even more serious face, the one he'd used at the funeral.

'We sent Mr Entwhistle over to the Isle of Man last year with his daughter, after Mrs Entwhistle died. Do you remember Mrs Entwhistle from church? They thought it was marvellous. We don't send everybody there though. Oh no. It's such a special place that we like to keep it a bit of a secret.'

'I don't care if it's a secret, I'm still not going.'

'Why don't you have a look at this?' He handed me a shiny coloured booklet. 'Have a look at the brochure and

I think you'll change your mind.'

He got to his feet and Dad showed him to the front door. As soon as they were out of the room I threw the brochure across the floor. Barney picked it up and started looking at the pictures.

'Wow! Check out this train! Look at the little steam engine!'

I told him to shut up.

'And look at this cat. It's got no tail!'

I grabbed his hair. 'I told you to shut your face.'

Matt was on me in a flash. He put his arm round my neck. 'You shut *your* face. We want to go on this holiday so keep your whingeing gob shut.'

Matt released me as soon as Dad came back into the room. He flicked through the brochure with Barney.

'Are we staying in a hotel?' asked Matt.

'A guest house,' said Dad. 'The vicar is sorting it out.'

'How long does it take to get there?'

'The train to Liverpool is about an hour.'

'Are we going on a train?' shrieked Barney.

'And the crossing is about four hours, I think.'

'What's the crossing?' asked Barney.

'The sea crossing.'

'The sea? Are we going on a boat?'

'A ship.'

Barney screamed 'Yahoo!'

'I'm not going on a ship,' I said.

'What are you going to do then?' said Dad. 'Walk across the water?'

Matt rolled up the brochure and bashed me over the head with it.

'Is baby frightened?' (Bash) 'Is he?' (Bash) 'Is he?'

I snatched the brochure from him and ran to the door.

'Get lost! Get lost the lot of you!'

I charged up the stairs and flung the brochure across the bedroom. It smacked into the wall and slid to the floor. I collapsed on my bed and cried myself to sleep.

chapter 13

Billy and Neville took me to the swimming baths. They were going to teach me how to swim in case the ship sank.

The pool was full of shiny, slippery wet bodies. Dozens of kids were splashing, jumping and ducking. Shouting, laughing and screaming. A fat boy was sitting quietly on the edge of the pool carefully pulling a plaster from his big toe. The plaster was caked in dry blood. He flicked it into the water.

A sharp whistle sounded. A man in shorts and a tight white t-shirt was pointing at us.

'Three to a cubicle!'

'Who's he?' I said.

'He's supposed to be a lifeguard,' said Billy. 'He's meant to save people from drowning, but all he does is chat up the birds.'

We crammed into the tiny changing space and Billy lent me a pair of swimming trunks.

'No trumping in them,' he said.

I asked Billy and Neville if they'd ever seen anybody drown.

'My great, great, great, great granddad saw hundreds of people drown,' said Neville. 'He was on the *Titanic*. When it sank he was the only person that survived.'

'That's rubbish,' said Billy.

'How do you know? You weren't there.'

'Because the only person on the *Titanic* who didn't drown was a woman called Mary Celeste. Everybody else went down to Davy Crockett's locker.'

I hung my clothes on one of the hooks. 'What's Davy Crockett's locker?'

'The bottom of the sea. Nobody comes back from there.'

We sat on the side of the pool and dangled our feet in the water. It was freezing.

'There's one thing to remember when you're learning to swim,' said Billy.

'What's that?'

He looked at Neville and they both started chanting:
'Remember, remember the golden rule,
Don't look down when you're peeing in the pool,
Keep a smile on your face like a happy fellow,
Then swim like mad before the water turns yellow.'

Billy leaped to his feet and dived in. Neville held his nose, jumped in and swallowed the fat boy's plaster that was floating on the water.

'Hello, Samuel.'

Miss Stern was standing next to me. She was wearing an orange bikini and an orange swimming cap.

'Hello, miss.'

When Billy saw her he zipped through the water and climbed out of the pool.

'Me Tarzan! You Jane!'

He started acting daft by wobbling his muscles. Neville got out and did the same. The lifeguard saw what was going on and whipped off his t-shirt. He really was a muscle man. Loads of kids clambered out of the pool and rushed towards him, cheering and shouting. In the stampede somebody knocked me into the water.

Frantically I flapped my arms and kicked my legs,

but I couldn't stop myself from sinking. My feet touched the hard tiles at the bottom of the pool. I flapped and kicked my way back to the surface. I could hear cheering and laughing. Then my ears and my mouth and my nose filled with water. Down I went again. I knew I was drowning and I knew that nobody else knew. The tiles were there again. Back to the top. I gulped in some air and let out a weedy shout for help. Then I sank to the bottom of the pool for the final time.

'Samuel, Samuel.'

I could hear somebody calling my name.

'Samuel, Samuel.'

I saw a flash of red above the surface. It was his jacket. I could see his rippled face staring down into the water from above. He was an old man. He was wearing a hat. A three-cornered hat. It was the man from the book in the hospital. William Hillary. The man who saved drowning sailors. He was leaning over the side of the pool, reaching towards me. I grabbed his hand and the next thing I knew I was clinging on to the metal rail at the side of the pool. Rubbing my stinging eyes, I looked around for the old man. He was gone.

Everybody else was still watching the muscle show as if nothing had happened. Suddenly, somebody had hold of my ankle. I looked down and caught sight of Dad in the water. He had a huge stone tied around his neck. He was drowning and he was trying to take me with him. As I slipped below the surface I screamed at the top of my voice.

'MUM!'

Then I woke up. I was still in the bedroom. I hadn't been to the swimming baths at all. It was a bad dream. And yet it had seemed so real.

It was dark now. I tugged the curtains across the window

and lay down again. It was very quiet. I couldn't hear the others downstairs. There was no noise from the TV, no talking. There were no cars on the lane. The bedroom felt cold. So cold it made me shiver. Then I smelled something. Lily of the Valley. I reached under the bed for the tin of talcum powder and emptied a few specks of the white dust into my hand.

Suddenly a thin beam of bright, white light shot through a tiny gap in the curtains. I watched the light move slowly down the wall. It stopped on the Isle of Man brochure lying open on the floor. I got to my feet, walked over to it and bent down to pick it up. The light became brighter and sharper and picked out one line of writing at the top of a page:

'Some people call it the Isle of Man. Others know it as heaven on earth.'

At first, I didn't understand. I didn't know what was happening. Then I remembered my prayer. God had finally decided to listen to me!

'Thank you,' I whispered.

Barney burst through the door and turned on the light.

'Dad says if you want anything to eat you've got to go and get it now. It's beans on burned toast again.' He saw me staring at the brochure. 'What's the matter?'

I told him to shut the door.

'Why?'

'Shut the door.'

Barney did as he was told. I sat on my bed.

'What's up?' said Barney.

'I'm going to tell you something and you've not got to tell anyone else. Promise?'

'Promise.'

'Cross your heart.'

'Cross my heart and hope to die, if I break this promise

I get no pie. Tell them *what*?'

'This place where the vicar is sending us …'

'What about it?' said Barney.

'It's heaven on earth.'

'What are you on about?'

'I kept saying I didn't want to go. The vicar told me to look in the brochure. Have a look at this and I think you'll change your mind, that's what he said. He was trying to tell me without letting the rest of you know.'

'Know *what*?'

'That it's heaven on earth.'

For a moment I was worried I'd said too much. What if this was meant to be private between me and Donald Duck? Had I already said more than I should? I decided it was too late – I'd told Barney half of it, so I might as well tell him the rest.

'I said a prayer, Barney. I asked God to let me see Mum so I could say sorry. My prayer has been answered. That's why the vicar has arranged for us to go to heaven on earth.'

'I don't get it,' said Barney. 'How can heaven be on earth? Heaven's in the sky.'

'*Proper* heaven is in the sky,' I explained. 'But this place is heaven on earth.'

'I've never heard of it.'

'It's secret. Donald Duck said they keep it secret because it's special, didn't he? Not everybody knows about it.'

Barney sat down next to me. 'Why is it secret?'

'It must be the place where people go just after they die. Before they ascend to proper heaven. Jesus did that, didn't he? One minute he was dead on the cross, next minute he was wandering round the garden as right as rain. In heaven on earth. He said ta-ra to everybody and then he ascended into proper heaven in the sky.'

'Jesus was special,' said Barney.

'Mrs Entwhistle wasn't special.'

'Who?'

'That old woman from church. When she died the vicar sent Mr Entwhistle and their daughter to this place.'

'Why?'

'So they could see her for one last time, I guess. And say goodbye. Now he's sending us there.'

Barney didn't know what to say. I put my arm around his shoulder.

'We're going to see Mum again, Barney.' I wanted to shout it from the roof top. 'We're going to see Mum again!'

chapter 14

I gazed up at the ship tied alongside. It was awesome. Higher than a house and ten times as long. The lower half was painted shiny black, the top was a gleaming white. Flags were flapping frantically from the two towering masts, one at either end. Between them was a big red and black chimney which Dad said is called a funnel. I was shaking. Possibly because I was nervous, but probably because it was the most amazing thing I had ever seen in my entire life.

Dad, Matt and Barney had already crossed the gangplank and were standing on the ship waiting for me.

'Come on!' shouted Dad. 'Get on board!'

I grasped the handrail and edged my way across the rickety bridge. Way down below, the dirty water was slapping against the side of the ship and sloshing around the slimy wooden pillars of the dock. One false move and I'd be in Davy Crockett's locker before we'd left Liverpool.

We made our way to the top deck, leaned over the side and watched the other passengers boarding below. I wondered how many of them were like me – off to see someone who had died. I wondered how many of them were like Dad and Matt – with no idea where they were *really* going. Barney had asked me if we should tell them. I said no. I figured if the vicar had wanted them to know about heaven on earth he would have let them in on the secret as he had done with me. It was my prayer that had been answered. It was me that was going to see Mum again. Me and Barney.

Suddenly there was a deafening blast from the steam whistle on the side of the funnel. A stream of thick black smoke poured into the air. Sailors scurried about the dockside loosening the fat ropes holding the ship alongside. They threw them on deck and set us free. We were moving. Ever so slowly we were drifting away from the dockside. Down below, the ship's engines stirred into life and the propellers frothed up the filthy brown water.

'I thought the sea was supposed to be blue,' said Barney.

'It is,' said Dad. 'This is a river. The Mersey. In an hour or so we'll be surrounded by the deep blue sea. Just us with a few white horses for company.' (That's what you call the foam on top of a breaking wave.)

Two long lines of rusty buoys marked our way along the river. One had a bell that clanged eerily as it rocked to and fro in our wake. For a while, a flock of seagulls escorted us on our way, dipping and diving excitedly around our heads. Eventually they fell away and headed back to Liverpool.

The ship was picking up speed and rolling ever so slightly; the water beneath us was getting deeper. That's when I saw the top of a ship's mast poking through the surface.

'Look!' I screamed. 'A sunken ship! What shall we do?'

Dad laughed. 'That old wreck has been down there for years, you daft devil.'

'What if *we* sink?'

Dad didn't answer.

'What will we do?'

'We're not going to sink.'

'We might hit some rocks!'

'We won't.'

'But what if we do?'

'Calm down!' Dad sat on a wooden bench and lit a cigarette. 'If we get into difficulty, which we won't, the captain will send out an S-O-S.'

'What's an S-O-S?'

'A radio message to alert other ships in the area. That's what you send if you're in trouble.'

'What if the radio doesn't work?'

'They'd use Morse code,' said Matt. 'Wouldn't they, Dad?'

'What's Morse code?' I asked.

Dad explained. 'It's a way of sending messages using sounds or lights.' He rapped his knuckles on the bench. 'Dot, dot, dot, dash … dash … dash … dot, dot, dot.'

'What does that mean?'

'It's Morse for S-O-S.'

I banged it out on the deck with my heel. Dot, dot, dot, dash … dash … dash … dot, dot, dot.

'What if nobody heard it?'

'They'd shout "abandon ship!"' said Matt. 'They've got lifeboats on here, I've seen them. Women and Sam first!'

'What would happen if you got in a lifeboat and that started to sink as well?'

'That's not very likely,' said Dad.

'But what would you do?'

'You'd do whatever you could to attract attention. You'd put your shirt or something on the end of an oar and wave it in the air.'

'What if – '

'Stop asking daft questions.'

'You'd better have this, Sam.' Matt was examining

a lifebelt fastened to a side rail. It was shaped like a huge Polo mint. Written on it were the words *Manxman, Douglas.*

'What does Manx mean?' asked Barney. 'What does it mean, Dad?'

'Anything from the Isle of Man is Manx.'

'Is there a Manx man called Douglas?'

'No, stupid. *Manxman* is the name of the ship.'

'How can a ship be a man?'

'A ship is never a man. A ship is always a lady.'

'Why?'

'Lots of reasons.'

'Like what?'

'Because she needs a master to keep her in trim.' Dad took a long, slow drag on his cigarette and a trail of smoke drifted from his nostrils. 'And because she's a thing of beauty,' he added quietly.

We went below deck to the galley where Dad bought a cup of tea for himself and three bottles of Pepsi for us. We sat at a table and Barney pulled a pack of cards from the duffel bag.

'Who wants to play Snap?'

I had a game with him, but Dad told us off for shouting.

'Give me the cards,' he said. I thought he was going to put them in his pocket, but he started dealing them. Four hands of seven cards each. 'I'll show you how to play a proper game. I played this all the time when I was at sea.'

It was called Rummy. It was a bit complicated, but once we'd got the hang of it it was really good. Dad won every game, of course.

By the time we went back up top the ship was rolling more than ever and it was hard to walk in a straight line.

Dad was right, the sea was blue and the white horses had appeared just as he had predicted. Every so often the wind blew sea spray into my face. If I licked my lips they tasted of salt.

'I'm hungry,' said Barney.

'Do you ever think of anything apart from your belly?' said Dad.

We followed him along the deck as he looked for a good spot for us to have our butties. He stopped when he found some deckchairs.

'Let's sit here and be posh,' he said.

Dad and Matt and Barney sat down, but I stayed standing and held on to a rail.

'This doesn't feel very posh to me,' said Matt. 'My seat's as hard as a rock.'

'It's posh because we're on the port side of the ship,' said Dad. 'That's the left side as you face the bow. Years ago when rich passengers booked their cabins on luxury liners they always asked to be on the port side for the outward journey.'

'Why?' asked Matt.

'Because it got more sunshine. On the homeward journey they wanted to sit on the starboard side.' Dad waved his arm towards the other side of the ship.

'Why?'

'So they got the sun again. Port out, starboard home. If you were rich, you always insisted – port out, starboard home. It got abbreviated on the passenger list to p-o-s-h. Posh.'

Dad took some sandwiches out of the duffel bag and he and Matt and Barney started feeding their faces.

'Do posh people have jam on their butties?' asked Barney.

'It's not what's on your butties that's important,' said Dad. 'It's where you're sitting when you're eating them, that's what counts. Today we're posh.' He shoved a sandwich in my face. 'Hurry up or there'll be none left.'

'I don't want any,' I said. 'I feel sick.'

'Don't worry,' said Matt. 'It's only two miles to the nearest land.'

'Which way?'

'Straight down.'

The vomit shot out of my mouth. It danced on the wind before zipping through the air and spraying up the back of an old man in a black raincoat. He didn't know anything about it.

'What shall we do?' said Barney in a panic.

'There's only one thing we can do,' said Dad. He got to his feet.

'Run!'

He grabbed the duffel bag and ran along the deck, laughing. Matt and Barney chased after him, they were laughing too. I wiped my face and went after them. They were hiding out of sight of the old man.

'I hope you said sorry to Joseph,' said Matt.

'Who's Joseph?'

'That fella with the coat of many colours!'

The three of them started laughing again.

'I'm going to the loo,' I said.

Dad was having hysterics. 'It's a bit late for that!'

I didn't really want to go to the loo – I just wanted to get away from them. I edged myself down a flight of steps, clinging on to the wooden rail as I went. I made my way along a corridor and opened a heavy door. The wind whipped it out of my hand. I stumbled forward over a metal step and fell on to the soaking deck. I was at the front of the ship. The sharp end. The door slammed shut behind me. I tried to get to my feet, but the roll of the ship sent me scurrying to a side rail. I grabbed it gratefully.

'Not found your sea legs yet?' The old sailor smiled through his bushy white beard. 'Don't worry, we'll soon be there.'

He led me by the hand to the flagpole at the very front of the ship. There he lifted me on to a ledge and held on to me. The wind was battering my face and my hair felt as if it was going to blow off. Waves were thumping against the ship and the spray was coming right over the top. It was terrifying. It was fantastic!

'On a clear day you'd be able to see the island by now,' shouted the sailor. He pointed ahead to a thick curtain of mist. 'But Manannan is wearing his cloak today.'

'Who is ...'

I could hardly speak because the wind was taking my breath away.

'Who is Manannan?'

'The god of the sea. Whenever the island is shrouded in mist they say he's wearing his cloak so as to keep the island out of sight of unwanted visitors. It's a special place for special guests, but don't worry, he's expecting you.'

The *Manxman* pushed on towards the mist. Nearer and nearer until it swallowed us up. Now I couldn't see anything in front of me and when I turned round I could only just make out the rest of the ship. It was only then I realised the sailor was no longer there. I was alone, but somehow I felt safe.

A deep moaning horn sounded in the distance and a big light flashed some way off. The wind was dropping and the sea was calmer. The *Manxman* was slowing down, gliding majestically through the stiller waters. A seagull swooped out of the mist and landed on the handrail a few feet away. In its beak was a single white feather.

'Is that for me?' I said.

The fat bird waddled towards me. I took the feather. The bird let out a piercing shriek and as if by magic dozens of seagulls appeared above my head squealing and screeching.

Suddenly the island was there! I could see purple-headed mountains and rich green hills. Beneath them a town stretched right around a huge bay fronted by brightly coloured buildings shimmering in the brilliant sunshine.

The *Manxman* edged her way towards the harbour. Perched above it on the rocks was the lighthouse that had guided her home. Sailors took up their positions and prepared to dock as the *Manxman* moved gently towards her berth and slumped, exhausted, against the gigantic tyres hanging along the side of the huge stone pier. We'd made it. We'd made it to heaven on earth!

chapter 15

We went in a taxi!

'Where to, boss?' asked the driver.

Dad checked the scrap of paper on which Donald Duck had written the name of the place we were going to stay.

'Paradise House, please. Mona Terrace.'

We sped through the narrow streets like VIPs being whisked to a secret hideout. Within minutes the driver dropped us off and wished us a nice stay.

We stood on the pavement and gazed up at the big house peering down at us. It was in the middle of a row just like our house at home, but it was much more grand. It was four storeys high, the brickwork was the colour of vanilla ice cream and all the window frames were Manchester City blue.

We began to climb. Firstly some steps from the street, through a wooden gate, more steps and then up the long front garden which was on a steep slope. Yet more steps to the front door which had a little bench outside.

Dad was puffing and panting as he plonked the suitcase on the patio and lined us up for inspection. He gave a click of his fingers for Matt to tie a shoelace and one for me to tuck my shirt into my pants. He gave Barney his handkerchief to wipe his nose before knocking on the door. None of us spoke as we waited for an answer.

I think we were a bit nervous. We were about to stay in somebody else's house. Somebody we'd never met.

The door was answered by a girl who was about eighteen years old. She had mesmerising green eyes and long dark hair tied back with a yellow ribbon that matched her summery dress. When she smiled she showed the whitest teeth I've ever seen.

'Hello, you must be the Bracegirdles,' she said with an Irish accent. 'I'm Kerry, lovely to meet you.'

She held out her hand and Dad shook it.

'Very pleased to meet you, Kerry,' said Dad who, for some reason, was speaking in a posh voice. 'I'm Jack and this is my eldest, Matthew. This is Samuel and my youngest, Barnabas.'

'Hello boys. Come on in.'

We stepped through the porch into a huge dining room that had six tables set for a meal. In the centre of each table was a vase filled with fresh flowers. Their smell hung in the air.

'Mrs Angel has popped out for a while,' said Kerry. 'But if you'd like to follow me, I'll get you settled in.'

Kerry led us into the hall where Barney pulled me to one side.

'Did she say Mrs Angel?' he whispered.

I nodded. 'I told you this was heaven on earth. Now do you believe me?'

We passed a door marked 'Kitchen' and followed Kerry up a long, wide staircase, every inch of which was covered in thick carpet. At the top of the house Kerry unlocked room 7, showed us into the large bedroom and gave the key to Dad. I ran to the big window.

'You can see the sea! Look, Barney, you can see the *Manxman* in the harbour.'

Barney was too busy inspecting the room.

'Can we put our things in these drawers?' he asked.

'You certainly can,' said Kerry.

He turned the little key in the door of the wooden wardrobe and had a look inside. 'Can we use this as well?'

'Yes, it's just for you.'

He sat in the small armchair by the window. 'Is that sink just for us?'

'Exclusively. And the bathroom and WC are down the corridor.'

'What's the WC?'

'The lavatory.'

'The what?'

'The bog,' said Matt.

'Wow!' said Barney. He ran to the bedroom door. 'Let's go and have a look, Sam.'

'There's no need to do that,' said Dad. 'We've all seen a WC before.'

'Not an indoor one,' said Barney.

Dad bit his lip and gave Barney a look which, when translated, meant 'belt up'.

'There aren't enough beds in here,' said Matt.

He was right. There was one double and one single.

'One of you will be in room 8 along the landing,' explained Kerry. 'Would you like to go in there, Mr Brace-girdle?'

Dad thought about it. 'No thank you,' he said. He put one hand on Barney's head and the other on mine. 'I'll keep an eye on these two. Matt, you can go in the other room.'

'Nice one,' said Matt.

'I'll show you where it is,' said Kerry.

She made her way on to the landing with Dad and Matt behind her. Dad was still trying to sound posh.

'Thank you very much. Much obliged.'

Barney gave me a puzzled look. 'Why is Dad talking

like Lord Snooty?'

'That's what happens if you sit on the port side for too long.'

Matt's bedroom was at the back of the house and it was nowhere near as good as ours. It was tiny with just a single bed and a little wardrobe.

'This used to be a big double room,' said Kerry. 'Mrs Angel had it made into two smaller ones last year. The dividing wall is a bit thin, I'm afraid. Don't worry if you hear a strange noise in the night, it will be Mr Silver snoring.'

I gulped. 'Mr Silver? That's the name of the man that took my tonsils out. Is he ... is he a doctor?'

'No,' said Kerry. 'I think he's a butcher.'

'He was a butcher as well!'

Kerry smiled. She didn't seem bothered that there might be a mad man staying in the house and that he was probably there to chop off various parts of my body.

'I'd be very grateful if you would do me a favour, Matthew,' said Kerry. 'When you get up in the morning could you give Mr Silver a knock? He hasn't brought an alarm clock and he can't see his watch properly. To be honest I think he should wear glasses.'

'It is him!' I said. 'The man who took my tonsils out should have worn glasses. Once he did the wrong operation and – '

'Please shut up about it,' said Dad as politely as he could.

'Make yourselves at home,' said Kerry. 'Dinner is at five-thirty.'

'We've had our dinner,' said Barney.

Dad smiled at Kerry. 'He means we've had our luncheon. Dinner at five-thirty will be lovely, thank you.'

As Kerry went downstairs Dad whispered to Barney. 'While you're here, your tea is called dinner and your

dinner's called luncheon, okay?'
     'Okay. So long as we don't miss out on supper.'

chapter 16

As soon as we'd unpacked we went outside to explore. We walked down to the seafront where the sun was glinting on the water and the waves were breaking gently against the promenade.

Dad breathed in through his nose and puffed out his chest before gradually blowing the air out of his mouth.

'Get a load of that,' he said.

I sniffed up. 'I can't smell anything,' I said.

'Exactly. It's called fresh air. Fill your lungs and take it back to Manchester.'

The four of us did just that, dragging it in through our nostrils and holding on to it as long as possible before reluctantly letting it go again.

We queued up to ride on a tram that was pulled by a horse. It was nearly full when it arrived and when it was our turn to get on there were only two empty seats. The conductor told Dad and Matt to sit in them and then he took me and Barney to the front and allowed us to sit next to the driver. It was brilliant, but we were very near the horse's bum and the air wasn't quite so fresh there.

We went in a huge joke shop in a place called The Arcade. It was jammed full of tricks and novelties – exploding cigars, powder that makes you itch and cushions that make a noise like a trump. There were plastic bluebottles, moustaches, fangs and sausages. Matt wanted to buy a plastic dog turd, but Dad wouldn't let him.

We watched a man making sticks of rock in a sweet shop. Each one had a little picture of three legs running through the middle. Dad said it's a special crest for the Isle of Man. We looked in the souvenir shops and those three little legs were everywhere – on wallets, key rings, tea towels, thimbles, mugs and spoons. You name it, it had three legs on it.

Auntie Betty had given us each 50 pence holiday money. Me and Barney both bought a pair of binoculars and Matt got a transistor radio. It had a tiny earplug which meant only he could hear it!

There's a street lined with amusement arcades and we went in one called The Golden Nugget. I've never seen or heard anywhere quite like it! The place was a dizzy mix of spinning fruits and flashing coloured lights with sirens sounding and buzzers buzzing. Above all of this was the constant clatter of cash. I won 4 pence on the Penny Falls, but I put it all back in and lost the lot. Matt kicked the machine to try and make some of the coins fall over the edge, but a bell started ringing. A woman came out of the Change Kiosk and told him off. Dad knew nothing about it – he was busy arm-wrestling with the Mr Muscles machine. It printed out a card that said he was puny. Dad laughed, but I think he was annoyed.

Then we had a game of bingo. Dad sat in the plastic seat and we huddled round as he showed us how to play. We took it in turns to slide the little black shutters across the numbers as they were called. My heart was pounding as we waited and waited for number seven. When it finally popped up Barney screamed and Dad leaped to his feet and shouted 'house'. Barney chose a bucket and spade for a prize.

At twenty past five Matt, Barney and me were sitting in a line on the edge of the double bed ready for dinner. Dad had made us change our shirts and wash our hands while he'd polished our shoes.

'I don't want to give you a long lecture,' he said. 'So I'll put it simply in plain English. If you show me up at the dinner table, I'll paralyse you.'

At half past five a gong sounded down in the hall. We ran to the bedroom door, but Dad made us wait five more minutes. We then had to walk slowly down the stairs like civilised human beings.

The other guests were already in the dining room. They were all adults – there were no other kids staying there. Kerry showed us to the one empty table by the window.

'I've put you here near Mr and Mrs Fenton.'

An old man and woman were sitting nearby.

'Good evening,' said Dad, as if he dined there every night.

'Good evening,' said Mr Fenton, with a nod of the head and a smile from the wife.

Barney gave me a nudge. 'Look,' he whispered. 'There are five chairs at our table. Is Mum coming for dinner?'

There were five knives and forks as well. Five cups and saucers and five napkins.

'Why are there five places at our table, Dad?' I asked. 'Who is the extra one for?'

'It must be for Mr Silver.'

My heart sank. 'Mr Silver? We don't want him sitting with us.'

Barney asked Matt if he'd seen him.

'No,' he said. 'But he *is* the doctor from the hospital.'

'How do you know?'

'I stuck my head round his bedroom door and saw a shirt lying on the bed. It was covered in blood from his operations.'

Kerry flitted among the tables giving everybody a bowl of soup.

Matt whispered to Dad. 'Is that all we get? Soup?'

'That's your starter. When you've finished it, you'll get your main course.'

I'd never seen soup like it. It had rice in it as well as vegetables. Dad said it's called minestrone. It was very nice and I would recommend it.

Barney used the wrong spoon and Dad told him off quietly.

'Use the other one,' he whispered. 'And use this, please.'

He handed Barney a thick cloth napkin.

'It's posh here isn't it?' said Barney. 'You even get a free snot rag.' He blew his nose on the napkin. Dad nearly died of embarrassment.

I took a piece of bread from the plate in the middle of the table. 'It's *very* posh,' I said. 'They've got triangle-shaped bread. Can we get some triangle bread when we get home, Dad?'

'They don't sell it round our way,' said Barney.

'Have you seen what they've got in the loo?' said Matt. '*Soft* bog roll!'

Barney was on his feet in a flash. 'I'm going for a pooh!'

Dad spoke through closed teeth like a bad ventriloquist. 'Sit down!'

Matt was first to finish his soup. He put down his spoon, picked up his bowl and licked it clean. Dad was about to tell him off when Mr Fenton leaned over from the next table.

'You enjoyed that, didn't you? Good for you! If you

can't enjoy yourself on holiday when can you enjoy yourself, eh?'

Dad forced a smile.

Mr Fenton slurped a mouthful of soup from his spoon. I thought old men only ate like that in cartoons, but this guy was for real. He guzzled another mouthful and it was even louder than the previous one. Barney deliberately did the same. He slurped his soup as noisily as possible and then looked at Dad with a wicked glint in his eye.

'I can't help it,' he said. 'I've got a wobbly tooth.' He lowered his voice. 'I think Mr Fenton has as well.'

Mr Fenton picked up a slice of bread, dipped it into his soup and sucked on it, noisily. Barney copied him. He knew there was no way Dad would be able to tell him off. Dad tried to pretend it wasn't happening. He picked up one of the two silver pots in the centre of the table and tried to pour us all a cup of tea, but all that came out was water. Kerry could see that Dad was getting flustered.

'Is everything all right, Mr Bracegirdle?' She looked in his cup. 'Oh, that's your hot water, sir, to top up your pot. Pass me the teapot and I'll be mother.'

We all looked at her and she realised what she'd said. Her pale cheeks turned ever so slightly rosy.

'I'm sorry,' she said. 'I wasn't thinking.'

We had steak and kidney pie with roast potatoes for our main course. Mr Fenton didn't eat any of his dinner and his wife had a go at him under her breath.

'You'll cause offence if you leave it,' she hissed.

'You eat it then,' he said.

So she did. That was followed by apple pie and ice cream. Mrs Fenton had two helpings of that as well.

Just then a little old lady came into the dining room. Her cheery face was tanned and wrinkled like an old leather armchair.

'Good evening everybody,' she shouted.

All the guests answered together. 'Good evening, Mrs Angel!'

'Have you all had a lovely day?'

'Yes, thank you, Mrs Angel!'

She came over to our table.

'You must be the Bracegirdles. Welcome to Paradise House. I hope you enjoy your stay.'

Dad thanked her very much and said he was sure we would. They had a chat about the weather and the crossing.

Barney tugged my sleeve. 'She doesn't look much like an angel to me,' he whispered. 'I thought she'd have a halo and a pair of wings, not an apron and a pair of slippers!'

'This is heaven on earth,' I said. 'Angels look different here. Besides, you can't expect her to cook the dinner wearing her angel outfit. How would she look with minestrone soup all down her robes?'

'So when do we get to see Mum?' asked Barney.

'Soon.'

'Where will she be?'

'In a special place, I guess. For new arrivals.'

chapter 17

After dinner we went on a coach tour. Me and Barney had the best seats – at the front near the driver. His name was Ken and he told jokes over the microphone.

'Why has a milking stool only got three legs?' he asked. 'Because the cow's got the udder!'

Ken knew everything about the Isle of Man. He showed us a church called St Trinian's which was built a long, long time ago. When the builders had finished it, some mischievous creatures came in the night and took the roof off. This happened time and time again and eventually the builders gave up and the church has remained roofless ever since. He showed us a hill called Slieu Whallian. In the olden days the villagers used to put women in a barrel full of spikes and roll them all the way down. If the women were still alive at the bottom of the hill they were witches.

After an hour or so we drove along a quayside towards a huge castle.

'And this, ladies and gentlemen, is the historic city of Peel, our destination for this evening. We'll stop here to stretch our legs and take refreshment.'

The sun was going down behind the castle and it looked as if somebody had smudged the sky with a thick orange crayon. We went for a stroll along the beach and Dad showed us how to skim flat pebbles on the flat sea.

We watched the fishing boats being tied up for the night before having a look in some of the shops.

'Who fancies a cuppa?' asked Dad.

'In a café?' I said. 'You mean a cuppa in a café?'

That's exactly what he meant.

The smell of coffee hit me in the face as soon as we opened the door. A man in a striped apron was making it by frothing up milk with a noisy machine. Another machine was full of chilled orange juice and another, with a picture of giant strawberries on the front, was for making milkshakes. There were blackboards behind the counter listing all the sandwiches, drinks and snacks that you could buy.

When I saw the expensive prices I was worried Dad would change his mind, but he didn't seem bothered – probably because church was paying. He picked up a tray and slid it along the huge counter past the cakes and buns and every kind of chocolate biscuit that's ever been invented.

'Can I have a milkshake, Dad?' asked Matt.

'If you say please.'

'Please.'

'Can I have one as well please?' I asked.

'And me,' said Barney. 'Please, please, please.'

The man in the striped apron poured Dad's tea from a huge shiny pot and told us to sit down while he made the milkshakes. I chose a table by the window.

Dad took three small envelopes out of his pocket. 'I forgot to give you these,' he said. 'They're off the vicar.'

Barney ripped open the envelope with his name on it. 'Wow! Fifty pence!'

Matt did the same and pocketed his cash. 'Nice one,' he said.

I took the coin from my envelope. It was unlike any I'd ever seen.

'Mine's not real,' I said.

Matt laughed. 'The vicar's slipped him a dodgy coin.'

'It's Manx,' said Dad. 'It's a Manx coin.'

'There's a note with it,' I said. 'Listen to this:

"Dear Samuel,

You will need to spend this money while you are there. It is special money for a special place.

Kind regards, Reverend Cook."'

'What's he on about?' said Matt. 'Special money for a special place. What does he mean?'

I realised the message was part of the secret and I shouldn't have read it out in front of Matt and Dad. I quickly slipped the note into my back pocket with the strange coin and changed the subject.

'Here come the milkshakes!'

At that moment Ken the coach driver came into the café. He got a cup of tea and sat at a table by himself. I had an idea. I waited until we'd finished our drinks and Dad and Matt had gone to the loo.

'Follow me,' I said to Barney. 'Ken's an expert. If any one knows where we can find Mum, it's him.' We went over to his table.

'Excuse me,' I said.

'Yes, young man?'

'Can you tell us where we have to go to see dead people.'

Ken put his cup down. 'Dead people?'

'Yes.'

'You mean a graveyard?'

'No, we went there when we were at home. This is a special place where you get a chance to see people again after they've died.'

Ken shook his head. 'I've never heard of anywhere like that, young man. Sorry.'

Barney and I wandered slowly back to the coach.

'I thought you said he was an expert,' mumbled Barney.

Ken didn't do any commentary on the way home – I think he was concentrating on his driving because it was growing dark. A few old women started a sing-song. 'On Mother Kelly's doorstep …; I'm a Lassie from Lancashire …; Show me the way to go home, I'm tired and I want to go to bed …'

We didn't join in.

When we arrived in Douglas Ken thanked everybody for their company and wished them an enjoyable holiday. He placed his cap on the dashboard and the passengers dropped money into it as they got off the coach. Dad threw in a handful of coins.

'Thank you,' he said. 'Most enjoyable.'

'Nice one,' said Matt as he jumped down onto the pavement.

Me and Barney were about to get off the coach when Ken called after us.

'Hey lads, I've been thinking. That place you're after, I think I know where you mean.'

He handed me a little book called *The Douglas Weekly Diary*. 'All the details are in there. You can have it if you like.'

'Thanks,' I said.

He winked. 'I hope you find the person you're looking for.'

I was dying to look in the book. So was Barney, but I told him we'd have to wait until Dad and Matt were out of the way.

chapter 18

When we got back to Paradise House Dad said we could go in the TV lounge for half an hour before bed. Me and Barney said we weren't interested and he could hardly believe it.

'It's a colour telly,' he said.

I told him we were tired and he handed me the key to our room.

'Go and get ready then. I'll pop up in a minute to check on you.'

We shot up the stairs, put on our pyjamas and slipped between the smooth fresh sheets of the double bed. I eagerly flicked through *The Douglas Weekly Diary* with Barney hanging on my every word.

'"Star Studded Stage Show at the Talk of the Town ...; Karma the Lightning Hypnotist at the Villa Marina ...; All Star Wrestling at the Lido ..."' Then I found it. 'Here it is! Listen! "You thought you might never see them again, but they're all here under one roof! Laurel and Hardy, President Kennedy, Marilyn Monroe – "'

'Does it mention Mum?' asked Barney urgently.

'"... And many, many more. Your chance to see them all again at – "'

'Lights out.' Dad was standing by the door with his finger over the switch.

'We're reading,' I said.

'You can't read in the dark.'

'It's not dark.'

Dad flicked the switch. 'It is now.'

'I want to go to the WC,' said Barney.

Dad switched the light on again and Barney dashed out of the room. Dad closed the curtains and sat on the bed beside me.

'What are you reading that's so interesting?'

I showed him the cover. 'It tells you what's on.'

'So what's on then?'

I opened *The Diary* and read the first thing that caught my eye. '"The Sound of Music" is on at The Picture House. Five p.m. and eight-thirty p.m. Matinee if wet. What does that mean? Matinee if wet.'

'If it rains they show the film during the day.'

'Can we go and see it?'

'We've not come all the way here to watch an old film.'

'It's Mum's favourite, she took me and Matt and Barney three times.'

'You don't need to see it again then, do you?'

'Why didn't you come with us?'

'I must have been working.'

'No you weren't. Mum said "Let's all go on a family outing", but you said you didn't want to.'

'Perhaps I was tired.'

'Can we all go on a family outing while we're here?'

'Yes, but not to see "The Sound of Music".' Dad pointed to the opposite page. 'Douglas Town Band is at the sea terminal building tomorrow night. That's more like it.'

Barney scurried back into the bedroom and dived onto the bed. A toilet roll popped out from his pyjama jacket and rolled across the bedroom floor.

'What are you doing with that?' said Dad.

'You said we could get some souvenirs to take

home.'

'Not toilet rolls.'

'But they're soft!'

'I don't care if they're solid gold, you're not stealing them.'

Dad picked it up, switched off the light and went downstairs. I waited for a couple of minutes and then nipped out of bed and switched the light on again.

'So where do we have to go to see Mum?' asked Barney.

I continued reading where I'd left off.

'"Your chance to see them all again at Louis Tussaud's Waxworks. They're all here, make sure you are too!"'

'Who's Louis Tussaud?' said Barney. 'And what's a waxwork?'

'Dunno, but Ken reckons that's the place. It says here it's on Wellington Street. "Open daily 10 a.m. to 4 p.m. including Sundays."'

'Yippee!' yelled Barney. 'We can go tomorr – '

'Shhh!' I put my hand over Barney's mouth.

A floorboard creaked on the landing.

'I think there's somebody outside our room,' I whispered.

Slowly and quietly I got out of bed and switched off the light. I opened the door slightly and peered through the crack. I was just in time to see a tall man in a long white coat going into the bedroom next to Matt's. I quickly closed the door and turned the key.

Barney was peeping above the bedclothes. 'Who was it?'

'I think it was Mr Silver.'

Suddenly a thin beam of bright light shot through a gap in the curtains and swept around the room. Then there was darkness again.

Barney sat up quickly. 'What was that?'

I ran to the window and flung open the curtains. A huge beam of light lit up one wall after another and then vanished.

'It's the lighthouse!' I shouted.

Barney let out a whoop of delight and I leaped back into bed. The whole room lit up again. Then darkness once more. Another sweep of light. Darkness.

'It's good here, isn't it?' said Barney.

'Yeah.'

We lay on our backs and watched the light show. It made me think of the 'curtain cars' back home and the night Mum had invented them. Me and Barney hadn't been able to sleep because we'd been frightened by an episode of 'Dr Who'. Mum made a chink in the curtains and stayed with us until the car headlights sent us to sleep.

'Dad said we can all go on a family outing,' I said. 'We'll take Mum to that café and buy her a milkshake. She'll like that won't she?'

Barney didn't answer. He was out for the count. I closed my eyes. The bed seemed to be gently moving up and down as if I was still at sea. The *Manxman* gently rocked me to sleep.

Some time later a noise woke me up. At first I couldn't work out where I was. Then the lighthouse flashed and I remembered I was in Paradise House. The noise was coming from the landing. Another sweep of light and I saw the door handle move up and down. Darkness. Somebody was trying to get into the room. I hid under the sheets.

'Open the door, Sam.'

I got out of bed, unlocked the door and let Dad in.

'Why did you lock it?' he asked.

'In case anybody tried to get in.'

'Who's going to want to get in, apart from me?'

I peered along the landing. Mr Silver's bedroom door was open a tiny bit. As Dad drew the curtains I closed our bedroom door and locked it quietly.

chapter 19

The smell of bacon climbed the staircase, crept underneath the bedroom door and woke us up. It was driving us round the bend, but Dad wouldn't let us go downstairs before seven-thirty.

Mr Fenton was already slurping his way through a bowl of Rice Krispies when we arrived in the dining room. I reckon he and his wife must have cheated and gone in there before the gong. Dad exchanged nods and 'good mornings' with them and we sat down at our table as the other guests drifted in for breakfast. Manx Radio was playing in the background and the weatherman told us we could look forward to an absolute scorcher.

An envelope was propped up against Dad's cereal bowl. He opened it and read the note in his head and then again out loud, quietly.

'Dear Jack and boys, welcome to the Isle of Man. I hope to see you all at St George's. Our service starts at 11 a.m. Yours sincerely, Reverend Parsons.'

Matt laughed. 'If he thinks we're going to church in our holidays he should be on "The Comedians".'

'It won't do us any harm to go,' said Dad.

We looked at him as if he'd just landed from another planet.

'You never go to church,' said Barney.

'Close your mouth,' said Dad politely. 'And eat your

breakfast.'

'I don't want it.' Barney pushed his bowl away. 'I don't like lemons.'

'It's not a lemon, it's a grapefruit.'

Very nice it was too. It was followed by cereal and then egg, bacon and sausage with a rack of triangle toast. Dad didn't say a word while he was eating, he was concentrating so hard. He cut a slice of toast into small squares and put a small piece of bacon on top followed by a piece of sausage and a bit of egg white. He dipped the whole lot in his yolk and then dabbed it in the brown sauce on the side of his plate. I tried to do the same, but everything kept falling off my fork. Finally, he wiped his plate with a triangle of toast, folded it in half, squashed the lot into his mouth and rinsed it down with a swig of tea.

'How was your breakfast, Mr Bracegirdle?' asked Kerry.

'Heavenly.'

Mr Fenton didn't eat his fry-up. When he thought nobody was looking, he switched his full plate with Mrs Fenton's empty one and she scoffed the lot.

'Why hasn't Mr Silver come down for his breakfast?' said Barney.

Matt nearly choked on his sausage. 'I forgot to give him a knock!'

'Go and do it now,' said Dad.

Matt pelted out of the dining room and up the stairs. He was back within seconds.

'Mr Silver's dead!' he gasped. Matt's face was white as a sheet. 'I knocked and he didn't answer! I went in and shouted at him, but he didn't budge! He's pegged it in the night!'

Dad, Matt and Kerry dashed up the stairs. Me and Barney raced after them. They crowded into Mr Silver's bedroom and closed the door. I opened it to try and see what was going on, but Dad closed it again. After a few minutes they all came out on to the landing.

'I'm sorry, Matthew,' said Kerry. 'I should have told you, he's a bit deaf as well as a bit blind. Perhaps tomorrow you might shake him as well as shouting at him.'

Dad followed Kerry down the stairs muttering an apology.

Barney quizzed Matt about the mysterious Mr Silver. 'What does he look like?'

'He's seven feet tall with bulging eyes and rotten teeth,' said Matt. 'And he talks in his sleep. I can hear him through the wall and it's pretty scary stuff.'

'Why? What does he say?'

'Something about an operation he's going to do. I think he's planning to sneak into somebody's room when they're asleep and cut them open.'

Barney gave me a look of sheer terror. I tried not to look scared.

After breakfast Dad, Matt and Barney followed me to church. I'd quickly planned a route using the little street map in *The Douglas Weekly Diary*. Dad had no idea I was taking him on a huge diversion.

As we passed the end of Wellington Street, me and Barney went into a little chat we'd practised before leaving Paradise House.

'Hey, look!' I said. 'A waxworks. I've always wanted to go in one of those.'

'Me too,' said Barney. 'Ever since I was little. Can we go in, Dad? Please.'

Dad didn't stop walking. 'We're going to church.'

We were ready for that. 'Church doesn't start until eleven,' I said. 'We'll be too early. Why don't we pop into the waxworks for half an hour?'

Dad showed no sign of slowing up. I thought we'd blown it until Barney played a blinder.

'If we get there too early you'll have to talk to the vicar for ages.'

Dad stopped in his tracks and thought about it.

'Half an hour,' he said. He gave Matt a handful of coins and then lit a cigarette. 'You three go inside, I'll come and find you.'

Me and Barney followed Matt through the front door into the entrance hall. There was nobody about and it was very quiet and very smelly – sort of damp and dusty. I think it's called musty.

'It stinks in here,' said Barney.

'That's the smell of hot wax and burning flesh,' said Matt. 'Have you any idea what goes on in this place?'

We didn't answer so Matt explained. 'Dead people are brought here and their bodies are covered in boiling wax to preserve them. Look at him.'

At the far end of the hall an old man was sitting in a glass booth. We moved closer to get a better look. His skin looked very realistic and he even had hairs in his nostrils. His eyes were closed and a dribble of spit was hanging off his bottom lip.

'He looks the same now as the day he died,' whispered Matt.

Me and Barney peered through the glass at the old man.

'Don't stare at him,' said Matt quietly. 'You'll awaken his spirit and if you do he'll haunt you to your grave.'

'Who is he?' whispered Barney.

'Let's ask him,' said Matt.

'How can we if he's smothered in wax?'

'We'll use corpse code.'

'What's that?'

'Morse code for the dead. I'll try and make contact

with him. If his spirit has heard me he'll answer with the voice of the devil.'

Matt took a coin out of his pocket and gently tapped it against the glass.

Barney spoke so quietly I could only just hear him. 'Will he understand that?'

'Yeah,' whispered Matt.

Matt tapped again, but the wax man didn't answer.

'It's not working,' said Barney.

Matt took some more coins from his pocket. 'Perhaps he's Manx.'

'What difference does that make?'

'I need a Manx coin, then he'll understand me.' Matt held up a Manx penny. 'This should do the trick.'

He rapped it on the glass. The man opened his eyes and sat up sharply with a groan. Me and Barney screamed and shot out of there as fast as we could. We ran straight into Dad. He led us back inside where Matt was bent double with laughter. Dad took back the coins he'd given to Matt and gave them to the old man.

'One adult and three children, please.'

The man licked his lips and the dribble of spit climbed back into his mouth. 'That'll be twenty-five pence, please.'

chapter 20

'Main Exhibition this way.'

The sign was next to a cardboard arrow that was coming away from the wall and pointing to the floor.

We went into a large hall which had dozens of thick, dark curtains hanging from the ceiling. In between each of the curtains were the wax bodies. Firstly, The Beatles. Ringo was on the drums, the other three were playing guitars and looked as if they were singing.

'Are The Beatles dead?' asked Barney.

'No,' said Dad.

'I thought you had to be dead before they covered you in wax.'

'Some of the wax dummies will be dead people,' said Dad. 'But some will still be alive.'

Barney looked to me for help, but I was just as confused as he was.

James Bond was there in his suit and bow tie surrounded by stacks of dusty gold bars. Bobby Moore was holding up a plastic World Cup and Neil Armstrong was standing in a crater made of papier maché.

Barney grabbed my hand and nodded his head towards a sign on the wall: 'You thought you might never see them again, step this way and be surprised.'

Just inside the small hall was a wax man with a big cigar in his mouth. Barney asked Dad who it was.

'Winston Churchill.'

'Who's he?'

'The Prime Minister during the war.'

'Is he dead?'

'Yes, he died years ago.'

Between the next two curtains was a man with a little moustache.

'Is it Charlie Chaplin?' asked Barney.

'It's Hitler,' said Dad.

'Was he in the war as well?'

'Yes, he started it.'

Laurel and Hardy were there in their black suits and bowler hats. Olly looked angry, Stan looked as if he was about to cry. We didn't know who any of the other wax people were so Dad had to tell us.

'That's John F. Kennedy, he was President of the United States … Marilyn Monroe, she was a film star … so was Errol Flynn.'

There was no sign of Mum.

'This isn't the right place,' whispered Barney.

I didn't say anything because I knew he was right.

'Nice one,' said Matt.

He was pointing to a sign written in dripping blood: 'Chamber of Horrors'.

'You're not going in there,' said Dad.

'Why not?' asked Matt.

'They might think you're one of the exhibits.'

Dad chuckled at his own joke as they went into the chamber. I didn't want them to know I was scared so I had no choice other than to follow.

It was dark inside – the only light came from fake flickering candles covered in real cobwebs. I tried only to look at the floor, but it was impossible to resist snatching a quick glance at the horrors all around – Frankenstein strangling a little old man, Dracula with blood dripping

from his fangs, a hooded axe-man beside a pile of sev-
ered heads. Matt had gone on ahead letting out 'oohs'
and 'aahs' of delight. Barney was behind him, echoing
with 'ewws' and 'arghhhs' of disgust.

'Mummy!' shouted Matt, pointing at an exhibit.

I hurried to see what he was looking at. Standing
between two curtains was a body wrapped from head
to toe in grubby bandages. It was an Egyptian mummy
like the ones I'd seen in a book at school. It wasn't grue-
some like everything else and I moved closer to have a
proper look. I studied the mummy's head. I could see a
pair of dark eyes staring back at me through a slit in the
bandages.

'Is there somebody inside those bandages, Dad?'

The eyes looked real and for a second I thought I saw
them move.

'Who is it, Dad? Is it somebody's mummy?'

I turned to Dad for an answer, but he wasn't there.
He'd gone. So had Matt. So had Barney. It was as if they'd
vanished into thin air.

'Dad? Barney?'

I could feel my heart thumping. I tried not to sound
frightened as I called out. 'I know you're hiding.'

I peered round the next curtain and came face to face
with a werewolf. I screamed and ran.

The place was a maze of curtains with somebody or
something lurking behind every one of them. I spotted
a door and barged through it – I thought it was the way
out – but I found myself in a small dark room. Along
each wall I could make out a row of ghostly figures. Wax
dummies had been covered with white sheets so their
heads and bodies were hidden and only their legs could
be seen. In the centre of the room I could see the silhou-
ette of a man. He appeared to be crouched on the floor
reaching out towards me. I fumbled along the wall and

switched on the light. It wasn't a real person – it was a model – a model of a drowning man. His head and one of his arms were above the papier maché waves. His face was fixed with a look of sheer terror. I recognised him immediately; it was the man from the cover of the book that the old lady had given to me in hospital. Lying on the floor beside him was a snapped wooden oar and a piece of rope.

At the feet of one of the covered dummies, was a hat. A three-cornered hat. I slowly walked towards the dummy, took a big breath and tugged at the sheet. It slid to the floor in a cloud of dust. Standing in front of me was William Hillary – the man who saved drowning sailors. The man I had seen in my dream – he'd grabbed my arm in the swimming pool. He was old, with white hair and wrinkled skin, but he wasn't feeble. He looked tough and strong and determined. He was wearing a bright red jacket and round his neck was a gold medal. I could just make out the words written on it: 'With courage nothing is impossible'.

Hillary's arm was reaching out as if he wanted to shake my hand. I slowly lifted my arm. I was trembling. I grasped his hand in mine. It was warm. I let go and ran to the door. I wanted to get out of there as fast as possible, but something made me turn back. The drowning man. The look on his face. I knew exactly how he felt and I couldn't leave him like that. I crouched down and pushed the drowning man across the room towards Hillary. Their outstretched hands met.

chapter 21

Dad marched through the church grounds like a man on a mission. Matt was a few paces behind, with me and Barney shuffling along at the rear.

'What are we going to do now?' asked Barney. 'How are we going to find Mum?'

I told him the truth. 'I've no idea.'

A woman was handing out hymn books in the church doorway. 'Good morning, welcome to St George's.'

Dad told her who he was and she took him to meet the vicar, who was standing by a notice board. The three of them had a chat.

Me, Matt and Barney wandered into the church and had a good look round. Most of the stonework was decorated with flashy gold squiggles, polished brasses gleamed on the altar and the bookstand was a huge golden eagle with a big Bible spread out on its wings.

'It's posher than our church,' said Barney.

He was right. There was no chewing gum stuck to the floor and no City players' names carved in the pews.

Dad joined us and we sat down near the back. During the service we didn't know when to stand up or when to sit down and we got it wrong a few times. We didn't know some of the hymn tunes so we just mumbled our way through.

The sermon lasted ages. The vicar's voice echoed

around the church. If you missed it first time round you caught it on the rebound. As much as I tried, I couldn't keep my eyes open, but I could still hear him droning on and on for what felt like hours.

'Behold I send an angel before thee! To bring thee into the place which I have prepared.'

Barney dug me in my ribs.

'Did you hear that?' he whispered.

I opened my eyes. 'Hear what?'

'Don't you get it?'

'Get what?'

'I'll explain later. Stay awake, this is important!'

The vicar rattled on for a while longer with Barney listening carefully to every word. So was Dad, which surprised me. Matt appeared to be paying attention, but he'd secretly slipped his earpiece into place and tuned in to Manx Radio.

Eventually the vicar ran out of steam. The sermon was over. After yet another hymn, an old man in a suit walked up to the big golden bird and gave a reading. It was all about storing up treasures and money and how it's a waste of time because someone will break in and nick it. Then it went on about how it's a waste of time worrying about what we're going to eat or drink or wear. Instead we should trust God and he'll give us all the treasures and food and drink that we need.

At the end of the reading the vicar fetched a huge gold plate from the altar and everybody instantly fumbled in their pockets and handbags for their wallets and purses. I suppose that's one way of making sure we don't store up any cash – take it all off us.

'Before the offertory hymn,' said the vicar, 'I am pleased to say that we have with us today some friends from St Peter's in Levenshulme, Manchester. They are Jack Bracegirdle and his three fine boys.' He gave us a nod. 'Welcome to the Isle of Man. We hope you find peace and comfort on our island.'

Dad didn't know what the offertory hymn was, but he got the hint when a man with a plate stood at the end of the pew. Dad pulled out the contents of every pocket. He hadn't got any coins. He looked to us for help, but there was no way we were parting with our holiday spends. Dad took out his wallet and produced a crisp five pound note. He turned to the man.

'Can you change a fiver?'

Me, Matt and Barney nearly died. The man's jaw dropped so far it nearly touched the floor.

Dad winked. 'Only kidding.'

At the end of the service Dad went to talk to the vicar again. Me, Matt and Barney went outside. Matt sat on a bench, listening to his radio. Barney dragged me along the path.

'We need to get back to Paradise House,' he said.

'Why?'

'Did you hear what the vicar said in his sermon? He said he'd sent us an angel to lead us to the place.'

I had no idea what Barney was going on about. 'What do you mean?'

'The place where Mum is! An angel will tell us where it is!'

'Mrs Angel,' I murmured.

'Exactly. When somebody needs help they always get a message off an angel!'

As soon as Dad came out of church we told him we were hungry and asked him if we could go back to Paradise House for something to eat.

'No need.' He tapped the duffel bag on his shoulder. 'Mrs Angel has given us a packed lunch.'

'Can we eat it now?' said Barney.

'And then we can go back to Paradise House,' I added.

'We can go back later. Come on, I don't want to eat my lunch in a graveyard.'

Dad headed for the gate and we all followed. We passed rows and rows of gravestones. Big stones, small stones, clean stones, dirty stones. 'In loving memory', 'ever loving memory', 'dear memory'.

'What are all these stones for?' asked Barney.

'So we won't forget people that have died,' said Dad.

'Why didn't Mum have one?' I asked.

'She will soon. It's being made specially.'

'What writing will it have on it?' asked Matt.

'Hannah Bracegirdle. Much missed by her loving husband and three sons.'

Barney pointed to a massive stone tomb with railings around it. It was by far the biggest in the whole grave-yard.

'Can Mum have one like that? Whose is it?'

We wandered over and had a look. Dad read out the words on the big stone plate.

'To the Honoured Memory of Lieutenant-Colonel Sir William Hillary.

Baronet of Yorkshire, Essex and Isle of Man.

Born 1771. Died 1847.

Soldier. Author. Philanthropist.'

'What's a philanthropist?' asked Barney.

'Somebody who does good things to help other people,' said Dad.

'Mum was a philanthropist, wasn't she?'

'Yeah, I reckon she was.'

Matt and Dad and Barney went through the church gate. I read the rest of Hillary's memorial.

'He founded in the year 1824 the Royal National Life-boat Institution and in 1832 built the Tower of Refuge in Douglas Bay. Fearless himself in the work of rescue from shipwreck he helped to save 509 lives and was 3 times awarded the gold medal of the institution for great gallantry.'

A centipede crawled up to the lid of the tomb and wriggled inside.

Dad made us walk round the harbour and up about ten million steps to Douglas Head. From there Douglas looked like a model village spread out below. The harbour looked tiny and the ships like toys. The sea, as flat as a blue snooker table, stretched to the horizon. We watched through our binoculars as the *Manx Maid* set sail.

Then we collapsed on the grass and waited for Dad to hand out the food. Mrs Angel had given us all a ham sandwich, a cheese sandwich, a tomato, a hard-boiled egg and a slice of fruit cake.

'Is this a picnic, Dad?' asked Barney.

'Yeah, I suppose it is.'

'I've never had a picnic before. Have you Dad?'

'Not for a long time.'

'Did you and Mum have a picnic when you went on holiday?'

Dad nodded and then stretched out on the grass with his hands behind his head. As soon as me and Barney had finished eating we did the same. We lay there for ages in the sunshine.

'Are we sunbathing, Dad?' asked Barney.

'Yeah. I guess we are.'

'I've never been sunbathing before – have you, Dad? Did you and Mum go sunbathing when you went on holiday?'

Dad didn't answer.

I closed my eyes. The only sound was the seagulls calling in the distance. I dreamed I was lying on a raft, floating towards the horizon. In real life I would have been terrified, but in my dream I wasn't scared at all. I was as calm as the sea.

Matt's voice woke me up. 'What's that, Dad?'

He was pointing at a small building further down the hill. It looked like a round version of Dr Who's Tardis. A sign above the door called it 'The Camera Obscura'.

'It's a hidden camera,' said Dad. 'It probably gives you different views of the surrounding area.'

'Can I go and have a look?' asked Matt.

Dad took out his wallet and pulled out his second fiver of the day. 'Why don't you all go? Let me have a rest.'

Matt took the money. We raced down the hill, entered the strange building and paid the man in the doorway. It was cool and dark inside. So dark, in fact, that we had to stand for a while to let our eyes get used to it. We walked slowly round the large stone slab in the centre. It was divided into different sections. On each one was a big photograph that was being taken by a secret camera. They appeared to be moving pictures of what was happening outside. The one of the harbour was brilliant – the sea looked so realistic it made you want to touch it to see if you would get your hand wet. It was amazing. I asked Matt how they did it.

'It's not a camera,' he said. 'It's a periscope.'

'I thought periscopes were for spying,' said Barney.

'They are, look at them two!'

In the next scene we could see a man in a dark blue football shirt snogging a girl in the long grass.

'Does he play for Everton?' asked Barney.

'Yeah. And I think he's just scored,' said Matt, with a smirk.

The next picture was Douglas seafront – a horse was pulling a tram along the promenade. After that was a view right across the bay to a place called Onchan.

On the next picture we could see Dad sitting on the grass. His face was buried in his hands. I don't know if he was crying or praying. Or both. We stood silently in the darkness and watched him.

chapter 22

We got Dad to take us back to Paradise House by telling him we wanted to go on the beach and Barney insisted we wear the new red plastic sandals Auntie Betty had bought us. While Dad was looking for them we said we were going to the loo and slipped downstairs to get our message.

I knocked gently on the kitchen door. Barney was by my side. He looked as nervous as I felt.

'Come in.'

Mrs Angel was at the sink, scrubbing the biggest frying pan I'd ever seen. The other pans draining on the side were massive as well – it was as if she was doing the washing up for a giant.

'Hello, my darlings. Is there something you want?'

'Have you … have you got a message for us?' I asked.

'A message?' Mrs Angel wiped the soap suds from her hands with a tea towel. 'No, I haven't love. Were you expecting one?'

We nodded.

'I've got a custard cream if you'd like one of those instead.'

Mrs Angel reached a tin from a shelf and we both took a biscuit. 'And I've got a little job if you'd be good enough to help me. I always take my ring off to wash the pots, but it's rolled off the window sill and disappeared.'

I lay on the floor and spotted it under a cupboard. I was just able to reach it.

'Oh thank you, you are a good boy. I don't know what I'd do if I ever lost this ring, it's so, so special.'

'Why?' asked Barney.

Mrs Angel slid the gold ring on to her old finger and rubbed it gently.

'This is the ring Mr Angel gave to me on the big day … forty-eight years ago is it now?' She thought for a moment. 'Yes, I've been an Angel for forty-eight years.'

'How did you become an angel?' asked Barney. 'Did you have to wait for Mr Angel to give you a gold ring?'

'Yes, and he made me wait a long time.'

'Why? Weren't you good enough?'

Mrs Angel laughed and more wrinkles appeared on her already wrinkled face.

'Does Mr Angel give out lots of gold rings?' asked Barney. 'Does he make lots of people into angels?'

'No, the only other Angel that will be giving away a gold ring is Gabriel, if he ever gets round to it.'

Me and Barney looked at each other. I don't know whose mouth was open the widest.

'Gabriel?' I said.

'That's right,' said Mrs Angel. 'My son.'

'The archangel Gabriel?' said Barney, totally gob-smacked.

Mrs Angel smiled. 'That's what all the other children at school used to call him.'

'Is he here?' I asked. 'I bet *he'll* have a message for us.'

'I don't think he will,' said Mrs Angel. 'But we'll go and ask him if you like.'

Mrs Angel led us down the hall and knocked on a door at the back of the house.

'Enter.'

Gabriel was sitting in the corner of the room reading a book. He didn't have any robes or wings or anything like that, but he had curly blond hair and the bluest eyes I've ever seen. He was about twenty years old and looked like Alan Tracy (Thunderbird 3). The only light inside the room was coming from a lamp behind Gabriel's head and there was a golden glow all around him. He looked very angelic, but for his shoes – I don't think they'd seen a tin of polish for at least a month. I have to say I was shocked to see an archangel with such grubby footwear.

Gabriel put his book in his lap and spoke in a soft voice.

'Hello there, young fellows.'

Mrs Angel introduced us. 'This is Samuel and this is Barnabas.'

I said hello, but Barney got straight down to business.

'Have you got a message for us, archangel Gabriel?'

Gabriel roared with laughter. 'I haven't been called that for a few years!'

Mrs Angel smiled. 'I was just telling the boys how the children at school used to tease you about your name.'

Gabriel nodded knowingly. 'It was my father's idea to give me such a grand title,' he explained. 'And it was he who insisted we call this place Paradise House!' He laughed again. '"We are Angels!" he would proclaim.'

'"And we shall dwell in Paradise!"' added Mrs Angel.

They both chuckled.

'Have you got a message for us?' asked Barney, again.

'No, we haven't got any messages,' said Gabriel. 'Have we, Mother?'

Mrs Angel shook her head.

Gabriel stood up and filed his book among the hundreds of others on the sagging shelves all around the walls. Then he lifted the lid on a piece of furniture in a corner of the room. I thought it was some kind of cabinet, but it turned out to be a small organ.

'I shall give you a further example of my father's sense of humour,' he said. 'Which tune do you think he had taught me to play before I was six years of age?'

'Don't start that racket now,' said Mrs Angel.

'Just a quick verse,' insisted Gabriel.

He rolled up his sleeves and banged out a dodgy version of 'Hark The Herald Angels Sing'.

'Sadly,' he said 'I have learned only two further tunes since then. The second one is not quite so angelic.'

He started to play something from 'The Jungle Book'.

'That's enough,' said Mrs Angel. 'You'll wake the dead.' She closed the lid of the organ and headed for the kitchen. 'I've got to get back to my chores. See you later, boys.'

'And I'm popping to the newsagent's,' said Gabriel.

We followed him down the hall.

'I suppose you're going to ask me which newspaper I'm going to buy, aren't you boys? Go on, ask me which newspaper I'm going to buy.'

I didn't know what he was talking about, but I asked him anyway.

'Which newspaper are you going to buy, Gabriel?'

'*The Guardian*.' He ruffled my hair. 'So now you know, I'm a Guardian Angel!' He laughed and disappeared out of the front door.

Barney began to trudge up the stairs. He had tears in his eyes. 'What do we do now?' he mumbled. 'If the angels can't help us, who can?'

I had no answer. I wandered outside and stood on

the patio. I leaned on the railings and gazed out to sea. How were we going to find Mum? We'd tried everything we could think of and I hadn't a clue what to do next.

chapter 23

'What are you doing this afternoon?'

I hadn't spotted Kerry sitting on the little bench on the patio.

'Going to the beach,' I answered.

'You'd better make the most of this sunshine. There's going to be a storm, by all accounts.'

'Oh,' was all I could think of to say.

'Are you going to build a sandcastle?'

I shrugged my shoulders. I didn't know and I didn't really care.

'Do you think you could build a castle like that one?' Kerry pointed to the small castle standing in the sea in the middle of the bay.

I'd seen it before, but I hadn't taken much notice of it.

'Come here and I'll tell you about it.' She patted the empty space by her side.

I could tell she was trying to cheer me up so I sat on the bench and tried to look interested. It would have been rude not to.

'Doesn't the sea look beautiful?' she said. 'As calm as a mill pond, as they say. Looking at it now, it's hard to believe it could ever be any different, isn't it?'

I nodded. Kerry put her arm round me. She smelled of soap.

'Believe me, the sea can be vicious in these parts. To make matters worse the bay is riddled with huge, treacherous rocks. You can't see them when the tide is high. In days gone by dozens of ships were driven on to them and wrecked. Many sailors lost their lives.'

Kerry paused for a moment and then began her story.

'One night back in 1830 a paddle steamer, the *St George*, was anchored in the bay. A storm had been brewing all night and by the early hours it had whipped up into a frenzy. Huge waves battered the ship until she could take no more. Her anchor chain snapped and the fierce winds drove her onto those confounded rocks.'

Kerry withdrew her arm and leaned forward on the bench. She stared at the sea as if the drama was being acted out before our eyes.

'The *St George* was holed. Seawater poured into the lower deck. The crew was left with only one option, to fire distress rockets and pray that somebody would go to their aid.'

I knew somebody would answer their call and I knew who it would be, but I waited for Kerry to continue.

'A group of brave volunteers raced down the beach. They were led by a man called William Hillary. He'd have been about sixty years old at the time. With no concern for himself he set out with his crew in their tiny lifeboat.'

Kerry turned to me. 'Lifeboats in those days weren't like the ones you see now,' she explained. 'They were just big rowing boats really. It took the men a good while to reach the *St George* as they battled against the ferocious waves and the evil weather.'

Once again Kerry's eyes were fixed on the bay. 'Eventually Hillary managed to get the lifeboat alongside the *St George*, but disaster struck! The lifeboat was smashed first against the rocks and then against the *St George*, tossed about like a cork in a cauldron. Oars were lost or snapped, the rudder was ripped off and then, just for good measure, a huge wave swamped the lifeboat, knocking Hillary and two of his crew into the turbulent water. The lifeboatmen scoured the rough sea for their comrades. They spotted the two crewmen and dragged them back on board, but they could only watch in horror as another gigantic wave flung Hillary against the rocks then dragged him back into the sea.'

'Did he … did he drown?'

'No,' said Kerry. 'A miracle happened. A rope was hanging from the stern of the *St George* and somehow Hillary managed to grab hold of it and hang on until the crew could pull him on board. His chest was crushed and his ribs were broken, but he was alive. By now the *St George* was starting to break up on the rocks. Hillary ordered all hands on deck to find as many ropes as they could and the men quickly lowered themselves into the lifeboat below. Dozens of them crammed into the tiny vessel with only two oars between them.'

'Did they make it?'

'The lifeboat picked its way through the wreckage, riding the waves and skirting the rocks. Just when hopes were beginning to rise, catastrophe! A huge wave caught the lifeboat, picked it up, turned it over and emptied all the men into the freezing water. They were exhausted. They could do nothing but cling desperately to the up-turned boat. A mountainous wave was heading towards them …'

'What happened?'

'They say the sea respects no one,' said Kerry quietly. 'She must have respected Hillary on that night. The gigantic wave caught the boat and the men clinging on to it and tossed it over the rocks into calmer waters. More volunteers had come out and they picked up the men, every single one of them. Not one was lost.'

'What about Hillary? Was he okay?'

'He was given a gold medal for his bravery along with some of the other crew members, but that wasn't the end of the matter as far as he was concerned. He vowed that no more men were going to suffer because of those fiendish rocks.'

'So he built the castle?'

'Yes. On the very rocks that had caused so many tragedies. It was to be some form of haven, a place for those in peril. When it was finished a bell was installed at the top of the tower so that sailors in distress could sound the alarm, but then wait in safety until the rescue could take place in calm waters.'

I remembered the words written on Hillary's grave in the church grounds. 'In 1832 he built the Tower of Refuge in Douglas Bay.'

I asked Kerry if the castle was called the Tower of Refuge.

'That's right,' she said. 'Some say it got its name from William Wordsworth, a famous writer who lived many years ago. He came here once and wrote a poem. Part of it was about the little castle. "Blest work it is of love and innocence, a Tower of Refuge built for the else forlorn."'

'What does "forlorn" mean?' I asked.

'Helpless. It's a place for those that need help.'

A place for those who need help. Was this the special place we'd been searching for? Was *this* the message we'd been waiting for? The message from on high.

'Kerry ... are you an angel?'

'I beg your pardon?'

'Are you one of the angels?'

'No, no. I just help them in the summer.'

'Would you like to be an angel one day?'

Kerry laughed. 'That's a bold question for one so young as yourself, but since you're asking …' She leaned towards me and whispered in my ear. 'Since you're asking, nothing would make me happier, but I've just about given up hope of that dream ever coming true.'

'Why?'

'Gabriel barely seems to notice me these days. At one time I thought he was as keen as I. We spent many a lovely evening chatting out here. Then, like a true gentleman, he'd walk me home. On my days off we'd take our bikes and go for picnics in the glens. It was so perfect, as if it was meant to be. Then suddenly, he seemed to lose interest.'

Kerry looked sad. I decided it was my turn to do some cheering up.

'I know what you need,' I said.

'Do you?'

'Yes. What you need is a gold ring on your finger. I know about these things.'

She smiled, but she looked sadder than ever.

'I don't think there's much chance of that happening, Sam. I've been here three summers now and I don't intend spending the rest of my days waiting around for Gabriel.'

chapter 24

I was dying to tell Barney about the Tower, but I waited until we were on the beach and safely out of earshot of Dad and Matt. They were sitting in deckchairs. Dad was asleep and Matt was plugged into his radio. It was baking hot and none of us were wearing shirts. Me and Barney were kitted out in shorts and our shiny red sandals. Barney was digging furiously in the fine sand as if he was trying to reach Australia.

'I know where we have to go to see Mum,' I said quietly. 'I've had the message.'

He stopped digging instantly. 'Where? Who told you?'

'Kerry.'

'I didn't know she was an angel.'

'She's not, but she will be one day. Now she's passed on her first message Gabriel will give her a gold ring and make her into an angel, you'll see.'

'So where is it?' asked Barney eagerly. 'Where do we have to go?'

I pointed to the Tower of Refuge. 'There.'

'You must be joking! It's in the middle of the sea!'

'Keep your voice down!'

'How are we going to get there?' whispered Barney. 'We can't swim and you nearly drowned having your hair washed.'

'I don't know,' I admitted. 'But we've got to get there somehow. For Mum.'

'It's impossible,' said Barney.

'With courage nothing is impossible.'

I had a look through my binoculars and gave my report to Barney.

'The castle is built on rocks like Kerry said. It's as if it's on its own little island in the sea. There's a big round tower with a small round turret on either side. In between is a tall, thin oblong tower with a flag on top. I think there are slits in the walls for windows, but it's too blurred to tell. You can definitely go inside it. I can see an arched entrance.'

'Look! Over there!'

Barney was pointing to the left side of the Tower. I didn't need my binoculars to see the five rowing boats in the sea.

'Maybe we can get one of those and row to the Tower,' said Barney.

The thought of going out in a little boat made me feel sick.

'We don't know how to row,' I said.

'It'll be easy. And how else are we going to get there?' Barney pelted along the crowded beach. 'Come on!'

We dodged round and leaped over the bodies sprawled out on brightly coloured towels. One man shouted at us as we accidentally kicked a shower of sand onto his oily chest.

A man and a woman were stepping out of one of the rowing boats at the water's edge. A tall thin man with arms like Popeye's dragged the boat up on to a bank of pebbles and slung it alongside the six others, each with a different number painted on their bow.

'Excuse me,' said Barney. 'How much is it to get one of those boats?'

The boatman looked at us and smiled. 'It's normally twenty pence, but you don't have to worry about giving me any money, sonny.'

'You mean we can have it for free?'

'No, I mean you're not having one, you're not old enough.'

A man with a little girl gave some money to the boatman. He shoved a boat into the water and held on to it while they climbed in.

'How old do you have to be?' I asked.

'Older than you. So why don't you two run along and play with your buckets and spades?'

We trudged back along the beach.

'Do you think we'll ever get to see Mum again?' said Barney.

'Of course we will.'

'But everything always goes wrong.'

'It's like a test,' I said. 'We passed the first part by getting the message off an angel. That was your idea, you thought of that. Now we just have to pass the next part. We can't row to the Tower, so we have to work out another way of getting there.'

Barney stopped walking. '*We* can't row,' he said excitedly. 'But somebody else could! Let's ask Matt to take us, he's old enough to get one of those boats!'

'He'll never do it,' I said.

'He will if we pay him.'

We quickly counted out our life savings of 55 pence.

'We'll give him all of it,' said Barney.

'No, we need twenty pence to pay for the boat. That leaves thirty-five for his wages.' We raced along the beach. Dad was still flat out. Matt was clicking his fingers to the music only he could hear. I kicked his foot and he pulled out his earplug.

I tried to sound casual. 'Do you want to earn some

money?'

'What are you on about?'

'We've got a job for you and we'll pay you.'

'What job? How much?'

'If you take us to that tower in a rowing boat we'll pay you thirty-five pence. What do you say?'

'Get lost.'

'Please.'

'Go by yourself.'

'We can't,' said Barney. 'The fella said we're not old enough.'

'When did he say that?'

'Five minutes ago.'

'You're older now, aren't you? Go and ask him again.'

'Please!'

'It'll cost you a lot more than thirty-five pence.'

Matt went back to his music.

I put my hand in my back pocket and took out the little envelope that Donald Duck had sent me. My Manx 50 pence coin was still wrapped up in his note.

'Dear Samuel,

You will need to spend this money while you are there. It is special money for a special place.

Kind regards, Reverend Cook.'

I kicked Matt's foot again and he unplugged himself.

'Ready to up your offer?' he said.

I handed over the Manx coin and counted out the rest of his wages into his grasping hand.

He put on a stupid voice that was supposed to sound like a pirate. 'For a fist full of doubloons, I'd sail on the *Titanic*. Now lead me to my ship, you scurvy lads!'

chapter 25

The boatman was dragging boat number 21 out of the water.

'We're older now!' shouted Barney.

The boatman looked at him and sniffed. 'What?'

'You told us to come back when we're older.'

'Are you trying to be funny, sonny?'

I told the boatman to take no notice of him. 'We'd like to take one of your boats out, please. Our big brother here is going to be the rower and he's very big as you can see.'

The man looked at Matt. 'Have you ever been in a rowing boat before?'

'Yeah, loads of times,' lied Matt.

I had my fingers crossed behind my back as the boatman thought about it. Barney tried to hurry him along by offering him our 20 pence.

The boatman took the bait. 'I want you back here in half an hour sharp. I'm packing up soon.'

Boat 21 was pushed back through the pebbles to the edge of the sea. The boatman held on to it as we climbed aboard. Me and Barney sat at the stern while Matt perched on the little wooden bench in the middle. He grabbed the oars.

'I thought you'd done this before,' said the boatman.

'I have,' said Matt.

'Do you always face the wrong way?'

Matt turned round and the boatman pushed us into the water.

'God bless the sea and all who sail in her!' shouted Barney.

Matt kept missing the water with the oars. Then they went in too deeply and he could hardly get them out again. After five minutes we were only about ten feet from the shore – I could still see the sandy sea bed below us. By now Matt was flapping the oars up and down like a pair of wings.

'Ready for take off,' said Barney.

Matt ignored him, summoned all his strength and rowed so hard he fell off the bench.

'You're useless!' I said.

'I'd like to see you do any better!'

'Hurry up,' said Barney. 'We've only got half an hour.'

Matt clambered back into position and eventually got the hang of it. Our boat moved steadily through the water accompanied by Barney humming the theme tune to 'Captain Pugwash'. I kept my eyes fixed on the Tower, not daring to peer over the side and down into Davy Crockett's locker; the surrounding sea was getting deeper by the minute.

'I'm getting blisters,' said Matt. 'And the sun's burning my back.'

'Keep rowing,' said Barney. 'That's what we paid you for.'

The Tower which had seemed tiny from the shore was slowly growing bigger and bigger as we got nearer and nearer. Another five minutes and we'd be landing on the rocks. We were five minutes away from seeing Mum again.

'Sufferin' seaweed!' shouted Barney. 'Look at that!'

About fifty yards away was rowing boat number 7. She was adrift with no sign of anybody on board. Matt stopped rowing. The only sound was the gentle sloshing of the water against the side of our boat. It was eerie.

'*Mary Celeste*,' said Matt quietly.

'Who's Mary Celeste?' asked Barney.

'She was on the *Titanic*,' I said.

'*Mary Celeste* was a ship,' said Matt. Now he was a pirate again. 'She was found driftin' on the sea. Not a livin' soul on board. Nobody knows to this day what 'appened to her crew. Some say they were eaten by a giant sea monster.'

'Never mind that,' I said. 'Head for the Tower.'

'No way,' said Matt. 'Let's investigate!'

Matt turned hard to starboard and headed towards the other boat. He was rowing faster than ever.

'I claim salvage!' he yelled. 'Anything on board is mine!'

'Look out!' I shouted.

We were heading straight for *Mary Celeste*. We were going to ram her side on. Matt stopped rowing, but it was too late. We closed our eyes and gripped the side of our boat as we thumped into the ghost ship.

A girl screamed and sat up quickly. A man popped up beside her, he had no shirt on. His chest was bright red. He must have been lying in the sun for ages.

'Idiots!' he shouted.

'Sorry,' said Matt. 'It was an accident.'

The man grabbed hold of the side of our boat and leaned over to Matt.

'Have you been spyin' on us?'

Matt shook his head.

'I don't believe you,' said the man. He turned to me. 'Have you been spyin' on us?'

'No,' I mumbled.

He let go of our boat and put his shirt on. It was an Everton shirt and I realised it was the same bloke we'd seen snogging on Douglas Head. It wasn't the same girl though.

The man looked at Barney. 'What have you got to say, fart breath? Were you spyin' on us just now?'

Somehow I knew that Barney was about to open his big mouth and put his foot in it.

'Not just now,' he said.

'What do you mean?' said the man. 'Not just now?'

'We spied on you through the periscope on Douglas Head,' said Barney. 'We saw you snogging that other girl, but we weren't – '

The girl in the boat went berserk. 'What other girl?' she shrieked. She clenched her fists and thumped the man on his back. 'What other girl?'

The man didn't flinch. He looked at each of us in turn. He was livid, but he spoke quietly which made it even scarier.

'You little creeps. You're going to regret this.'

The girl was still knocking holes out of him. 'What other girl?'

The man grabbed one of our oars and dragged it into his boat. He went to grab the other one, but Matt got hold of the other end of it. They were both tugging at the oar. Our boat was rocking violently. I clung to the side, looked towards the Tower and started yelling.

'Mum! Mum!'

Barney did the same.

'It's no good shoutin' for your mummy,' said the man. 'She can't hear you out here.'

The man let go of the oar and Matt fell backwards over the little bench and banged his head. The man grabbed the oar again and pulled it into his boat. Now he had both of them.

'See how you peepin' toms get on now!'

He started to row back to the shore with our oars.

Matt struggled to his knees. 'Come back!' he shouted. 'Give us the oars!'

'Oh, sorry, do you want them?' shouted the man. 'Here you are then!'

He threw them into the sea. My whole body began to shake.

'What ... what ... what are we going to do? What ... what ...'

Matt thumped me on the arm. 'Shut up and start paddling.'

'It's too deep to paddle!'

'With your hands! Paddle with your hands!'

Matt leaned over the side and tried to use his arms like oars, but the boat didn't move. Barney had a go, but he could hardly reach the surface of the water.

'We'll never ... never get back to the land,' I stammered. 'It's m ... m ... miles away.'

'We're trying to get the oars!' shouted Matt.

'Let's get to the Tower of Refuge,' I said. 'That's what it's for, sailors in distress.'

'Don't be so stupid!'

'You're stupid,' I said. 'This is all your fault!'

'It's your fault, you wanted to come out here!'

'It's your fault for saying you could row!'

'It's your fault for being born!'

Barney joined in. 'It's both your fault ... yours faults ... it's both yours fault ...'

'Shut it you!' said Matt.

The three of us spent a few minutes telling each other to shut it.

'You shut it!'

'I said shut it first.'

'Both of you shut it.'

'You can shut it as well.'

'Shut it yourself.'

Then a few minutes saying nothing.

I tried to spot Dad on the beach, but it was too crowded and I didn't have my binoculars. The sun was hammering down, bouncing off the sea and scorching our bare backs.

'We're doomed,' I said quietly.

'I know what you're supposed to do in a situation like this,' said Barney. 'I know how to raise the alarm.'

We both looked to him to save the day.

'What you're supposed to do is wave your shirt on the end of an oar. It's a shame we haven't got a shirt. Or an oar.'

Matt was about to thump Barney when I pointed urgently towards the shore.

'Ship ahoy!'

The boatman was rowing towards us, his boat moving through the water like a torpedo.

'I'll throttle you lot!'

He fished our oars out of the water, flung them in our boat and made us follow him back. He was shouting and swearing all the way. He made us drag our boat over to the others and tie it up.

'Right!' he said. 'Now I want to see your mother. Where is she? Eh? I want to see her!'

We stomped off along the beach.

'Come back, I want to see your mother!'

'So do we!' I yelled.

Dad was still asleep. Matt plonked into his deckchair and plugged himself in. Me and Barney sat in the sand and stared at the Tower.

chapter 26

On the way back to Paradise House Dad called in a shop to buy a postcard to send to Donald Duck. The shop sold small plants. The sign in the window said they were Manx palms. Barney asked Dad if they would grow into real palm trees like you see on treasure islands.

'I guess so.'

'Can we get one?'

'I don't think they'll grow in our back yard,' said Dad.

'Can we? Please. We can plant it in Mum's little garden.'

'Yeah,' said Matt. 'It will be like a garden of remembrance.'

So Dad bought a plant and Barney carried it carefully along the prom. Dad walked beside him examining the leaves.

'No, it won't grow,' said Dad. 'The future doesn't look good.'

'How do you know?' asked Barney.

'I've just read your palm.'

He and Matt had a good laugh at that one. For a moment I was a bit jealous. Jealous of them laughing and joking and enjoying their holiday while me and Barney were busting a gut trying to find Mum. I was tempted to tell them all about it, but I kept my mouth shut.

We had chops with chips and peas for dinner. Mr Fenton didn't touch his. His wife was really annoyed with him and she tried to eat his as well as her own, but she was too full. There was no sign of Mr Silver as usual.

'Why doesn't he come down for any meals?' asked Barney.

'He's too embarrassed about his table manners,' said Matt.

'How do you know?'

'I saw him this morning outside the bathroom. He said it's not easy to eat if you've got a hook instead of a hand.'

Barney's eyes widened. 'Has he got a hook? Honest?'

'Yeah, and he said he's going to come to your room tonight and use it to take out your appendix.' Matt looked at me and grinned. 'And yours.'

I decided I was going to lock the door at bedtime and leave it locked until Dad came to bed.

Somehow Mrs Fenton managed to find room for her dessert. When she'd finished she gave her empty bowl to Mr Fenton and swapped it for his which was still full. She was about to tuck into her second helping of fruit cocktail when she saw us watching.

'They're such big portions, aren't they?' she sighed. 'I don't know if I can manage all of this, we had such a big lunch.'

'What do you mean, *we?*' snarled Mr Fenton.

As Kerry was giving us our dessert Gabriel passed through the dining room. He was reading a book. Barney shouted hello to him, but he walked straight out of the front door. Perhaps he didn't hear.

'Don't take it personally,' said Kerry. 'If he'd take his nose out of a book for one minute he might see that there are other people in this world.'

She seemed angry with him and she nearly spilled our little jug of cream.

Barney took forever over his dessert. He deliberately stretched it out in the hope that we wouldn't have to go to the band concert. It didn't work.

As we walked along the corridor of the sea terminal building Barney was still desperately trying stalling tactics.

'My shoe's come off,' he said feebly.

'Put it back on,' said Dad.

'Why can't we go on the crazy golf?' moaned Barney.

'Because we're going to listen to the band.'

We took our seats in a huge hall filled with row after row of old people. After a few minutes the conductor welcomed us all to the concert and promised us a wonderful evening of music beside the sea. He tapped his stick on his music stand, waved it in the air and the brass band burst into life. So did the old folk – tapping their feet, clapping their hands and singing:

'Oh, I do like to be beside the seaside,

Oh, I do like to be beside the sea,

Oh, I do like to walk along the prom, prom, prom

Where the brass band plays tiddly-om-pom-pom ...'

Matt put his earplug in. I wished I had one – with or without a transistor radio.

The conductor announced the band was about to play a selection of tunes that he was sure we would all recognise. Suddenly the hills were alive with the sound of music.

I whispered to Barney, 'Follow me.'

We got to our feet. Dad gave us a quizzical look that I answered by mouthing the word 'loo'. Me and Barney walked to the back of the hall and out of the door.

It was going dark outside. Dozens of seagulls were lined up along the sea wall, settling down for the night.

'Let's go and see the *Manxman*,' I said.

We went through a big iron gate and made our way along the Victoria Pier. There was nobody about and the only sound was the brass band in the distance – they were trying to solve a problem called Maria. Three ships were tied up alongside – *Manxman*, *King Orry* and *Mona's Isle*. Each had a sturdy chain at the bow which disappeared into the dark water. Deep down below a big anchor was making sure they didn't come to any harm in the night. The three of them were gently bobbing up and down as if they were nodding off after a tiring day at sea. The band played 'Edelweiss' as if it was a lullaby to send them to sleep. The Douglas Head lighthouse made its first sweep of the evening and every so often the beam of light lit up the ships. We gazed at the *Manxman*.

'Night, night,' I whispered. 'Sleep tight.'

Just then a breeze ran along the pier and caught the plastic cover stretched over a lifeboat on deck. It flapped in the wind and tapped urgently against the side.

'*Manxman* is answering,' said Barney quietly. 'In Morse code. What's she saying?'

I listened to the rapid dots and dashes. I didn't know what they meant, but I pretended I did.

'With courage nothing is impossible,' I said.

The breeze dropped and the *Manxman* was silent. We wandered back along the pier and leaned on the sea wall. A couple of seagulls took off and glided silently onto the water below. The sea looked black and the Tower of Refuge had lost its shape in the darkness. It looked like a cardboard cut-out.

'It looks as if there are more rocks around the Tower than there were this afternoon,' said Barney.

'Yeah. It's something to do with the tide. When the

tide goes out the rocks appear.'

'Who makes the tide go out?'

'Manannan. The god of the sea.'

'If he made it go right out, we'd be able to walk to the Tower,' said Barney. 'Perhaps we should ask him. Shall we say a prayer to the god of the sea?'

'We can't do that,' I said. 'The Bible says we're only allowed to have one God.'

'We'd only be praying to one god at a time. There's nothing wrong with that. Jason did it.'

'Jason who?'

'Jason and the Argonauts. Do you remember that film Mum took us to see? Whenever Jason was in a fix, he asked a different god to help him.'

'They weren't proper gods,' I said. 'They sat around all day drinking wine and eating grapes. Our God doesn't do that, he works hard.'

'Yeah, but today is his day off. What are we supposed to do if we need help on a Sunday?'

Barney put his hands together, closed his eyes and bowed his head.

'Our Manna Man, who art in heaven …'

He turned his head to me and opened one eye.

'Does Manna Man art in heaven or does he art in the sea?'

'The sea I guess.'

Barney returned to his prayer.

'Our Manna Man, who art in the sea, hallowed be thy name, thy kingdom come – '

'That's no good,' I said. 'His kingdom is the sea. We don't want the sea to come, we want it to go away!'

'Thy kingdom go away – '

'I'll do it.'

I climbed on to the sea wall and carefully got to my feet.

Barney was having kittens. 'Sam, what are you doing? Get down!'

As the band began to climb every mountain, I faced the sea and stretched my arms out wide.

'Manannan, god of the sea!' I shouted. 'If you can hear me, give us a sign!'

'Sam! Look!'

A string of fairy lights that was hanging between the two lampposts behind us flickered into life. We watched as the same happened with the next string of lights, and the next and next until the full length of the promenade right around the bay was twinkling in red and blue and yellow and green.

'He's listening, Sam. Manna Man is listening!'

'Manannan!' I shouted. 'We ask that you take away the tide so we may walk to the Tower! Do you read me loud and clear?'

Fairy lights came on all around the arched entrance.

'It's working!' shouted Barney. 'Yahoo!'

The band started to play 'Do-Re-Mi'.

I leaped forward and landed on a set of stone steps below, about half of them were above sea level.

Barney screamed.

'It's okay, Barney,' I shouted. 'It's okay.'

He dashed to the gate in the wall and ran down the steps to join me. The band was really going for it so we joined in:

'Soh - doh - la - fah - mi - doh - re ... '

As we sang, we jumped up and down the steps like the kids in the film, the sea sloshing round our feet.

'Soh - doh - la - te - doh - re - doh.'

When it came to my line, I didn't miss it this time. I sang at the top of my voice:

'When - you - know - the - notes - to - sing,
You - can - sing - most - any - thing!'

'Has he done it yet?'

Barney had his face pressed against the bedroom window, staring out to sea. I was looking through my binoculars. We'd been watching and waiting for nearly an hour. We'd got out of bed as soon as Dad had switched off the light and gone downstairs.

'I don't think so,' I said.

I could see the fairy lights at the Tower, but it was too dark to see the sea. It was even trickier when the lighthouse flashed in our direction.

'Why hasn't he done it?' said Barney. 'Why hasn't he made the tide go away?'

'These things take time,' I told him. 'I reckon he'll have done it by the time we wake up.'

'He'll have to,' said Barney. 'It's our last day tomorrow!'

A flash of lightning danced on the horizon and thunder rumbled far away. Barney's face was a mixture of terror and excitement.

'Is Manna Man doing that?' he asked.

'Yeah.'

Just then a floorboard creaked on the landing. Barney and I looked at each other and then at the bedroom door. In the next sweep of the lighthouse we saw the handle move and the door begin to open ever so slowly. I'd forgotten to lock it.

Barney grabbed my pyjama sleeve. 'There's somebody there,' he whispered.

'Shhh!'

We waited for the next sweep of light. The door was half open now. There was another rumble of thunder. In the flash of lightning that followed we saw the shadow on the wall. The shadow of a giant hook!

Barney was shaking. 'It's Mr Silver!'

We hugged each other, closed our eyes and waited

for the cold steel to pierce our trembling flesh.

There was a strange noise from the landing. I think it was supposed to be an evil laugh, but it sounded more like Basil Brush with a sore throat. I let go of Barney and crept to the door.

I quickly yanked it open with a scream, 'Wargghh!'

Matt jumped out of his skin and dropped a coat hanger on the floor.

'You idiot!' he shouted. 'You frightened the life out of me!'

I slammed the door in his face. Me and Barney looked at each other and burst out laughing. I ran to the wardrobe, grabbed a couple of coat hangers and we dived onto our bed. As the lighthouse flashed we made giant hook shadows on the wall. Outside, Manannan was really getting stuck in with the thunder and lightning.

chapter 27

I was woken by the wind lashing the rain against the front of the house.

'You won't get much of a suntan today,' said Dad, while he was shaving.

I got out of bed and tried to look out of the window, but it was hopeless – rain was pouring down the glass. Outside it was grey and dull – the sort of day that looks as if it's never going to get light. It was impossible to tell if Manannan had done the business or not.

Dad wiped the smudges of shaving foam from his face with a towel. He put on a shirt and said he was going to check that Matt had managed to wake Mr Silver.

'Can I come and help? Can I have a go at shaking him and shouting at him?'

'We don't need any help, thank you.'

'I just want to see him,' I said.

'Mr Silver is not a tourist attraction.'

He didn't show up for breakfast. Again.

Mrs Angel gave us black pudding with our egg and bacon. I don't like black pudding and Dad scraped it onto his plate. Matt suggested we should have given it to Mrs Fenton.

'She doesn't look as if she's got much to eat,' he said.

He was joking. She was already halfway through Mr

Fenton's breakfast.

Me and Barney stuffed our food into our faces as quickly as possible. We were dying to get to the seafront to see what had happened. Before that we had to work out how to get rid of Dad and Matt. We needn't have worried.

'I'm going to nip back to St George's this morning,' said Dad. 'I want to have a chat with the vicar.'

We looked at him as if he'd gone mad.

'You've hardly been to church in all your life,' said Matt. 'And now you're going twice in two days?'

'That's right,' said Dad.

'Why? What do you want to talk to the vicar about?'

'Something that was said in the service. That we shouldn't worry about money and how we're going to pay the bills. That's what I've done all my life. Perhaps it's time to change.'

'We don't have to go with you, do we?' asked Barney.

'Do you want to?'

'No way.'

'No chance,' I added.

Matt scratched his head. 'Let me think, do I want to go and have tea with the vicar on the last day of my holidays? That's a tough one.'

'There's no need to try and be funny,' said Dad. 'If you're not coming with me you can look after Sam and Barney. I'm making you responsible for them.'

Now all we had to do was work out how to get rid of Matt. I just hoped it wouldn't cost any more money because me and Barney were skint. Dad took some coins out of his pocket – it was as if he'd been reading my mind. He gave us each a 50 pence piece.

'Don't throw it all away in those amusement arcades.

In fact, don't go anywhere until it stops raining because I didn't pack your raincoats.'

Dad borrowed an umbrella from Mrs Angel and we watched from the bedroom window as he battled his way along the road. As soon as he was out of sight we dashed downstairs and out into the rain. We hopped, skipped and jumped over the puddles all the way to The Golden Nugget. By the time we arrived we were sopping.

Matt joined the crowd of steaming bodies at the Change Kiosk and eventually emerged with cupped hands full of coins.

I pointed to a sign on the wall: 'Children under 16 must be accompanied by an adult'.

'We're not allowed in here without Dad,' I said. 'I think we should leave. We might get into trouble.'

'You big baby!' said Matt. 'Where are you going to go? To watch the Punch and Judy show?'

'Good idea. Come on, Barney.'

We stepped out into the pouring rain.

'It won't be on in this weather!' shouted Matt. 'And you'd better be back here by twelve o'clock!'

We ran to the promenade. There were hardly any people about and those that were out had their heads down and their umbrellas up. A horse and tram went by. The horse was soaked and he looked really sad. There was nobody on board apart from the driver and the guard who looked thoroughly miserable in their hats and macs.

We darted across the road to the railings overlooking the beach. The wet sand stretched almost as far as the Tower.

'He's done it!' I shouted. 'Manannan's gone and done it!'

Barney was speechless.

We clung to the rusty metal handrail and picked

our way down the slippery stone steps on to the empty beach. It was hard to believe it was the same one that had been crowded with sunbathers the day before.

The Tower looked further away than ever. The first part of our expedition would be easy, it was simply wet sand. Beyond that the beach looked darker. I thought it might be seaweed, but hoped I was wrong – I'd seen a fair bit of that stuff when we were in the rowing boat and I didn't like the look of it. After that there was more sand, a pool of water and then the rocks.

I asked Barney if he was ready. He nodded.

'Let's go!' I shouted.

chapter 28

We charged down the beach, the wet sand splat-
tering up the backs of our legs and spraying on
to our soaking shorts and windjammers. We were two
tiny specks in the wide sweep of Douglas Bay which we
had to ourselves. We splashed through the huge puddles
of seawater dotted about the beach, they were only a
couple of inches deep and there was no point in going
round them – we were saturated already and the rain
was showing no sign of letting up.

Suddenly Barney stopped running and stared at his
feet.

'Eww! Look! Worms!'

I ran back to have a look. By now Barney was stamp-
ing on the long grey squiggles curled up on top of the
ridges in the sand. I don't know what they were, but
Barney had it in for them. Wet sand squirted out from
under his sandals. Neither of us was wearing socks and
our feet were now a muddy brown colour.

We'd only just started running again when Barney
stopped once more.

'Eww! Look at this!'

'Will you stop "ewwing" and keep moving?'

'What is it, Sam?'

Plopped in the middle of the sand was a gigantic jel-
lyfish. I'd never seen one before, but I knew that's what

it was. It really was like jelly, clear jelly with stringy blue and orange streaks inside.

Barney tried to move it with his foot. 'Is it dead?'

'Leave it! They can still sting you even if they're dead. Come on!'

We ran further down the beach and stopped at the edge of a massive bed of soaking seaweed. There were tons of it in every shade of green and brown that's ever been created. Some pieces had tentacles, some were weird flower shapes and others looked like a window cleaner's leather.

'I'm not going in there,' said Barney.

'You'll have to, there's no way round it. Come on.'

I closed my eyes and sank a foot into the mushy mess.

'What's it like?' asked Barney.

I've never stepped in chicken giblets, but I guess that's what they'd feel like. 'It's nice.'

'Liar.'

I put my other foot in and the seaweed squelched up to my ankles.

'There's nothing to be frightened of,' I said, worried that Barney wasn't going to follow.

I squidged further and further into the swamp. It seemed to get deeper with every step. It felt as if the seaweed was trying to wrap itself around my legs.

'Is seaweed alive or dead?' shouted Barney.

I didn't want to think about it. All I wanted to do was turn back, but by now I was halfway through the smelly sludge. Then I heard an 'eww' behind me and I knew Barney had taken his first step.

If he thought the seaweed was a problem, I had even more bad news. Ahead of us was another stretch of wet sand, but beyond that was water. What had looked like a small pool from the promenade was actually a moat of seawater around the Tower. It lay between us and the rocks.

Barney picked his way through the last of the seaweed and we ran to the water's edge. I couldn't tell how deep it was and wasn't sure we'd be able to wade through it.

'I thought Manna Man was supposed to have sorted this,' said Barney.

'It's only a moat,' I said. 'Every castle has a moat. If we paddle through this we'll have done it.'

I stepped into the chilly water. Barney followed me, but only for a few steps.

'Sam, it's getting deeper.'

'It's only up to my shins,' I said.

'Yeah, so that means it's up to my knees! Stop!'

I stood still in the water and wiped the rain from my face. It was the coldest I've ever been in my entire life. Suddenly the rain seemed to get heavier and the wind drove it at my skin like hundreds of tiny jabbing needles.

'Come on, Barney. We can't turn back now, we're nearly there! Once we're through this water we're on to the rocks and then it's easy!'

'It's too deep!'

'We don't know that!'

'I'm not going to find out!'

'I am!'

I strode further into the water. In no time it was up to my knees. Then it was touching the bottom of my shorts. As it reached my belly it took my breath away and I stood for a moment, gulping in the air.

'Sam, come back!'

'I'm not giving up!'

'What about me? Don't leave me!'

Barney's face and legs were bright red and his hair

was plastered to his head. His shorts and windjammer were stuck to his body and he was shaking from head to toe. I waded back to him and crouched down so he could climb onto my back. He put his arms round my neck and I set off again. I think the water was getting colder as it became deeper, I don't know – I couldn't feel anything any more. I pushed on. Now it was round my waist. Barney's feet were dragging along the surface making him seem even heavier.

'Turn back Sam, it's too deep.'

'If we can just get to the rocks we've made it.'

'I don't like it, turn back!'

I was staggering under his weight. Each step was becoming harder and harder. Then, as I lifted my foot, my sandal stuck in the soft seabed.

'My sandal's come off!' I screamed.

I was balancing on one foot.

'Don't drop me!' yelled Barney.

He was slipping round my back. He grabbed my throat.

'Let go! You're strangling me!'

I was toppling over.

'I'm going to have to put you down!'

'No!'

I put my bare foot on to the sea bed to stop myself from falling over. It was sandy, it was okay. I took another step and another. Suddenly it was sharp. A stone. Or was it a crab? Or a shark? Or Davy Crockett's fingernails scratching at my feet as he tried to drag me down to his locker? I closed my eyes, let out a scream of determination and stepped quicker and quicker.

'We're nearly there!' shouted Barney. 'We're going to make it!'

I opened my eyes. The huge rocks were only a few yards away. Perched proudly on top of them was the

Tower of Refuge. Suddenly it looked massive. The water level was down to my knees, my shins, my ankles.

'We've done it Sam! We've done it!'

Barney slid down my back and immediately began to climb a rock five times his size. I sat down and examined my foot. The skin was wrinkled as if I'd been in the bath for a month. My big toe was cut, but it was too cold to bleed.

'I'm the king of the castle!' shouted Barney from the top of the rock. 'Come on!'

I got to my feet and climbed after him. Every time I put my weight on my bare foot it was agony.

'Oww! Oww! Oww!'

'Will you stop "owwing" and get a move on?'

We were climbing over rocks that had dashed the ships of old and claimed the lives of dozens of sailors. The same rocks that holed the *St George* over a hundred years ago!

'Look at this!'

Barney had discovered a short stone jetty among the rocks. We clambered on to it. Ahead of us, at the end of the platform, was a mound of big pebbles. Beyond that was the arched entrance to the Tower.

'No!' screamed Barney. 'Look!'

The entrance to the Tower appeared to be bricked up. I staggered along the jetty, the rain bouncing around my feet. I stumbled over the pebbles to the Tower entrance. Inside the archway, tucked away to one side, was a short flight of stone steps.

'It's okay Barney! There are some secret steps!'

Barney ran to my side and we caught our breath in the calm and quiet of the Tower entrance. Then we looked up to the top of the short stairway. This was the moment we'd been waiting for. Nervously I called out.

'Mum? Mum, are you there?'

chapter 29

Barney took my hand and we slowly climbed the dingy stairway. It led out onto a stone platform between the two small round turrets. Between them was the entrance to the main Tower. We went inside. It was dark. It was damp. It was empty.

'There's nobody here,' said Barney.

'I can see that.'

We stood in the centre of the round Tower. There was no roof to protect us and the rain was coming down as fiercely as ever – it was everywhere, racing down the high circular wall that surrounded us and darting like arrows through the slits in the rough stonework.

'This isn't the right place,' said Barney. 'We've come all the way out here for nothing.'

'It *is* the right place.'

'So where's Mum?'

'She'll be here,' I said calmly. I sat down on the soaked, cold stone floor. 'We just have to wait.'

After a few minutes Barney sat down too. He scraped together a mound of tiny pebbles and threw them, one at a time, at the opposite wall. Plink … plink … plink …

I put my arms over my head and put my head between my knees to try and shut out the eerie whistling of the wind, but it was impossible.

After a while the plinking stopped – Barney had

thrown his last pebble. He got to his feet and faced the wall. I asked him what he was doing.

'What does it look like?'

'You're not peeing in here.'

'Why not? Nobody can see.'

'You're not doing it in here, go outside.'

'Get lost.'

I jumped up and grabbed his hair. 'Go outside!'

'Gerroff!'

Barney shrugged himself free and went to the top of the stairway. He stopped dead still and stared down the steps as if in a trance.

'Mum?' he gasped. 'Is that you?'

I darted to his side to see for myself.

There was nobody there.

Barney laughed. 'Made you look, made you stare – '

I put my hand round his throat and pushed him against the wet wall.

'This isn't a joke and you're not funny. Got it?' I cracked the back of his head against the sharp stonework and watched his eyes fill with tears. 'Got it?'

He'd got it. I let him go and he started crying.

'Where the hell is she then? Eh? Where the hell is she?'

The more he wiped the tears from his eyes, the more he cried. 'You said we'd see Mum again. You said this was heaven on earth. There's no such place and I'm going!'

'You can go to hell for all I care!'

I didn't think he'd go, but he did. As he ran down the steps I shouted after him.

'If you tell anybody where I am, I'll paralyse you!'

I went back into the main Tower, picked up a big pebble and slung it as hard as I could against the opposite wall. It bounced back and smacked me on the head. I sank to the floor, buried my head in my hands and began to sob.

'Mum, please come back. I love you and I'm sorry. Please come back.'

'Sam! Sam!'

Barney was calling from a distance.

'Sam! Come quick!'

'Get lost!' I shouted, though I doubt if he heard me.

'Sam, please!'

I wanted to ignore him, but he sounded serious and I knew he wouldn't mess about with that lump I'd given him.

'Sam! Please help!'

I got to my feet and trotted down the steps. As I passed through the arched entrance my heart began to pound. The tide was racing in. The moat around the Tower was much wider and I could tell it was deeper – waves were starting to break on the rocks and the stone jetty had gone.

'Sam!'

Barney was way over to one side of the Tower. He must have gone a different way back to try and avoid going through any deep water, either that or he'd completely lost his bearings. He was stranded on a tiny island of sand in the middle of the sea.

'Sam! I'm stuck!'

'Run!' I shouted.

'I'm scared!'

He was only in it up to his ankles, but between him and the shore the water looked much deeper and fiercer.

'Run Barney!'

He made a dash for it. He'd only taken six steps before the water was up to his knees, then his belly. He turned back to his little island. I think he tripped. Or slipped. I don't know. He disappeared beneath the water.

'Barney!'

I scrambled into the swirling sea. A wave crashed onto me and nearly knocked me off my feet. I clambered back on to the rocks gasping for breath. There was no way I would be able to reach him. I stood for a moment, waving my arms at the promenade and calling for help, but I knew it was pointless – there was hardly anybody about and if there had been I doubt they would have seen or heard me. Then I remembered the bell. Kerry had told me about a bell for sailors to raise the alarm. I shot up the steps and darted into the main Tower. About halfway up the circular stone wall was a small ledge which I guessed must lead to the bell tower above. I began to climb the wall. There was hardly anything to grab with my hands and when I tried to get a foothold my one remaining sandal kept slipping from the wet wall. I kicked it off.

In my head I could hear myself shouting at Barney. 'You can go to hell for all I care! You can go to hell for all I care! You can go to hell for all I care!'

'Shut up!' I screamed.

I was halfway up the wet wall. I could feel the ledge with my hands, but I had no idea how I was going to pull myself up.

That's when I had the spooky feeling. As if I was standing in the centre of the Tower looking up at myself clinging to the wall.

It was as if someone was there, taunting me. 'Look at you, you're pathetic!'

'Shut up.'

'Weed!'

'Shut up.'

'You're stuck, aren't you? Can't get up, can't get

down.'

'I'm having a rest.'

'Useless weed!'

'Shut it!'

I pressed my hands down on the ledge and yanked my whole body up as hard as I could, my feet and knees scraping against the wall. I managed to get my elbows on the ledge and pulled myself up inch by inch until I could get my right knee on to it. Then I slid my body into the tiny gap. There was just enough room for me to kneel down. I turned my neck and peered up the slim tower above my head. There was no bell!

I felt trapped. I could hardly breathe. It was as if the stone walls were closing in and going to crush me. I'd never be able to get out of there. I wouldn't be found for years; I'd become a skeleton huddled up in a tiny tomb. At first they'd think I was a sailor from the olden days. Then they'd realise it was me. They'd work it out from my bones.

'It's Samuel Bracegirdle! The famous weed!'

My back felt as if it was going to snap in two.

'Help,' I mumbled. 'Please help.'

'Jump!' screamed the voice in my head.

'It's too high.'

'You're pathetic!'

'I climbed up didn't I?'

'Jump down then!'

'I'm going to wait until somebody rescues me.'

'Nobody knows you're here.'

'They'll be looking for me.'

'They won't start looking for you until Barney's body is washed up on the beach.'

'Shut up.'

'Another one dead because of you.'

'Shut up! Shut up! Shut up!'

One foot must have hit the ground before the other. A pain shot up my right leg just before my head smacked against the stone floor. I lay still. A big pebble was lying on the ground a few feet away. It went blurred. Then clear again. Blurred. Clear. I reached out, grabbed it and banged it on the ground.

Dot, dot, dot, dash … dash … dash … dot, dot, dot.

And again.

Dot, dot, dot, dash … dash … dash … dot, dot, dot.

The walls were blurring now. I fought to keep my eyes open. I could hear the sea crashing against the rocks outside. It would be up to the Tower entrance by now, but I knew it would never come inside. I could hear Kerry's voice, as soft as a lullaby.

'A Tower of Refuge built for the else forlorn.'

My eyes were closed now. I just had the strength for one more try.

Dot, dot, dot, dash … dash … dash … dot –

Somebody was coming up the steps. I opened my eyes to see who it was, though deep inside I already knew. Standing at the entrance to the main Tower was William Hillary, the rain dripping from his three-cornered hat. In his arms was Barney.

Hillary stepped inside the Tower, laid Barney on the ground and knelt down beside him. Barney's eyes were closed.

I was almost too afraid to ask. 'Is he … ?'

'He's fine,' said Hillary. 'Cold and exhausted, but he'll recover soon enough.'

I struggled to my feet and limped to Hillary's side.

'Thanks,' I said.

He smiled. 'I am at your service.'

'Why do you save people?' I asked.

'We all have a choice. We can stand and watch others suffer, or we can reach out and help them. I could not stand by and watch somebody drown, could you?'

'I can't swim.'

'Nor can I,' he said quietly.

Hillary stood up. He was about to leave. I felt I had to tell him why we were there.

'We came here because ... because we thought ...'

'I know why you are here.'

'So ... is my mum here?'

Hillary placed a huge hand on top of my head. 'With courage nothing is impossible.'

I watched him walk quickly down the steps and disappear into the rain. I never saw him again.

I turned to check on Barney. Mum was sitting beside him caressing his head.

'Hello Samuel.'

I ran to her and flung my arms around her neck and buried my face in her hair.

'Mum, Mum, Mum,' I sobbed.

She held me close. 'Hush, my darling.'

'Mum, I'm sorry. I'm sorry.'

'You have nothing to be sorry for,' she said gently.

She took out her handkerchief, dabbed it on her lips and wiped away my tears. I sat down beside her and rested my head on her chest.

'You're a very brave boy, Samuel. I'm proud of you.'

Barney opened his eyes and gazed up at Mum.

'And I'm proud of you too, Barnabas.'

'Please don't go away again, Mum,' I said. 'Please stay.'

She lifted my head, turned it to face her own and looked me straight in the eyes.

'I will always be with you, Samuel.' She looked at Barney. 'And you Barnabas. I want you both to remember that. Wherever you are, whatever you are doing, I will be by your side.'

Barney just had enough energy to give Mum a smile before closing his eyes again.

'I love you, Mum,' I said.

She hugged me and I could smell the Lily of the Valley.

'Samuel, there's something I'd like you to do for me. I want you to look after your father. I need you to reach out and help him. I can no longer do it, but you can.'

I didn't understand. 'What do you mean?'

'A man does not need an ocean in order to drown,' she said.

'But … what do you want me to do?'

'Love him. That's all. Just love him.'

I snuggled up to Mum. In spite of the cold and the wind and the rain, she was warm. As always.

chapter 30

When I opened my eyes, I was curled up on the ground in the centre of the Tower. I was soaked to the skin and still the rain was coming down.

'Mum?' I said quietly.

I looked around. Mum was nowhere to be seen.

'Barney?'

He wasn't there. The place was empty.

'Barney?'

Then I remembered him disappearing beneath the waves. I sat up quickly.

'Barney!' I shouted.

I tried to get to my feet. My ankle was killing me.

'Barney!'

Barney staggered into the Tower. He was soaked and exhausted.

'I can … I can see a lifeboat,' he said.

'Tell them we're here, Barney. Quickly!'

He made his way back down the steps and I heard him calling for help. A few minutes later a lifeboatman appeared in a bright yellow coat.

'And you must be Samuel,' he said. 'How are you doing?'

'Okay.'

'Glad to hear it. Come on, let's get you back to dry land.'

He swept me off my feet and carried me down the steps, through the swirling sea to a big rubber dinghy. Barney was already sitting in it with another lifeboat-man who rowed us out to the Douglas lifeboat which was waiting in deeper water. The crew lifted us on board, wrapped us in blankets and we headed for the harbour.

The lifeboatmen carried us up the wet stone steps onto the pier where a crowd of people was waiting. One of them was Dad.

'Where the hell have you been?' he yelled. 'Come here!'

Me and Barney walked nervously towards him. He raised his arms. I thought he was going to bang our heads together. Instead he hugged us close.

'I thought I'd lost you too,' he said quietly.

An ambulance took us to hospital where a doctor checked us over and a nurse bandaged my ankle and put plasters on my toe and knees.

We got a taxi back to Paradise House where Matt was leaning out of our bedroom window watching for us. As we traipsed up the garden path he shouted and waved before dashing downstairs to meet us at the front door. He seemed really pleased to see us.

'Are you okay? What's happened to your ankle, Sam?'

I don't know if he was seriously concerned, but I must admit he's gone easy on me since that day. He hasn't hit me once and, best of all, he's never again said it was all my fault.

Mrs Angel made us some soup and sandwiches and the four of us had the dining room to ourselves. Barney was first to finish.

'What are we doing now?' he said. 'Crazy golf?'

Dad laughed. 'You two are having a hot soak and

going to bed.'

I had the first bath and then went to the bedroom to put on my pyjamas. As soon as I'd done that I crept back along the landing. As I passed the bathroom door I could hear Barney trying to convince Dad he didn't need a bath because he'd spent most of the day in water. It was an argument he couldn't win and Dad continued to fill the tub.

I sneaked down the stairs. I had some unfinished business to attend to.

I tapped on the door at the back of the house.

'Enter.'

Gabriel was glowing in the corner, reading a book as usual.

'Hello there young fellow,' he said. 'I've heard all about your exploits, how are you feeling?'

'Okay thanks.'

'That's good. What can I do for you?'

'Well … I know it's not normal for people to give messages to you … and normally you give them to us … but, anyway, she helped me so I'm helping her.'

Gabriel put his book down. 'You've lost me. Who are we talking about?'

'Kerry.'

'Kerry?'

'Yeah. You see … she wants to become an angel.'

'She what?'

'That's what she wants more than anything in the whole world, but she said you hardly notice her any more.'

'Kerry said that?'

'Yeah, and she said she's not going to spend all her life waiting for you to put a ring on her finger.'

Gabriel opened his mouth to say something, but nothing came out so I carried on.

'I reckon you're mad if you don't take her on, she's really nice. Don't you like her?'

He stood up slowly as if in a daze. 'Like her? I'm potty about her!'

'Well you'd better get a move on before you're too late.'

He moved swiftly to the sideboard and rifled through the top drawer.

'I thought it was the other way round,' he said. He was flinging papers and envelopes all over the place. 'I thought she didn't want anything to do with *me*.'

Finally he found what he was looking for. A tiny box. He opened the lid and showed me a gold ring.

'I was going to give her this on her last birthday, but I lost my nerve … I thought she … to tell you the truth, I was convinced she'd say no.'

'She's just waiting for you to ask,' I said.

As I went back up the stairs Gabriel played the organ. It was as bad as ever, but his singing was even worse:

'Zip-a-dee-doo-dah, Zip-a-dee-ay,

My, oh my, what a wonderful day!'

It's not the sort of behaviour I would have expected from an archangel!

I had to hold Barney up while Dad struggled to get him into his pyjamas – he was already asleep and kept swaying from side to side. Eventually Dad lifted him into bed and I climbed in next to him.

Dad closed the curtains. 'I think it's finally stopped raining,' he said.

I asked him if he thought the matinee would have been on at The Picture House. He didn't know what I was talking about.

'Matinee if wet, remember?'

'Yeah, I reckon so,' he said.

'How wet does it have to be before they decide to put it on?' I asked.

'I don't know.'

'What if it chucked it down all morning and the manager said the matinee was on, but then the sun came out. Is he allowed to change his mind and call it off again?'

'I doubt it.'

'What if it was sunny all morning, but then, right at the last minute, it suddenly started raining and the manager decided the matinee was on. How would he let everybody know?'

'I've no idea.'

'It's a good job you're not the manager, you wouldn't know what to do.'

'You're right there.'

'People would be wandering round in the street not knowing whether they're going to get to see the film or not. I reckon it must be the worst job in the world being manager of The Picture House. You'd have to spend all morning looking out of the window at the clouds and bobbing back inside every hour to check the weather reports on Manx Radio. I don't know why they don't just show the matinee every day, it would be much easier for everybody.'

Dad smiled, walked over to the door and switched off the light.

'Dad?'

'Yes?'

'I love you.'

Silence.

'Do you love me, Dad?'

'That's a daft question.'

'Whenever Mum put us to bed she always told us she loved us.'

'Well ... ' I could hear him fiddling with the door handle in the darkness. 'Women say those sort of things.'

'Are men allowed to say those sort of things?'

No answer.

'Are men allowed to say "I love you"?'

'You've gone barmy. Have you been drinking seawater? It sends you round the bend, you know.'

'I love you, Dad.'

'Go to sleep.'

'Okay. But I'll still love you when I wake up.'

He closed the door and went downstairs.

I climbed out of bed, went over to the window and opened the curtains. In the blackness I could see the fairy lights at the Tower in the middle of the bay. It was strange to think I'd been there. It was even stranger to think that the next day we would be going home to our house in our street. It seemed a million miles away. I felt as if I'd been on the island for months.

The lighthouse beam swept around the room as it would continue to do when we had gone.

chapter 31

When I woke, Dad was leaning out of the window having a cigarette. The suitcase was packed and waiting only for our pyjamas. Four pairs of polished shoes were standing by the door ready to go home.

I smiled at the thought of Gabriel's grubby footwear and remembered something Dad had once said: 'You can tell a lot about a person by their shoes.' I'm not sure he's right. I reckon it's the person wearing them that really matters.

I got up and got dressed. Dad woke Barney and while he was helping him to get ready I said I'd go and check Matt was awake. I hurried along the landing, but it wasn't Matt I wanted to see.

I knocked on Mr Silver's door. There was no answer. So I knocked again, very loudly. Nothing. I took a deep breath, turned the handle and pushed the door open. Mr Silver wasn't there. The bed was neat and tidy and looked as if it hadn't been slept in.

I barged into Matt's room. 'Did you give Mr Silver a knock? Did you wake him up?'

Matt sat up in bed and rubbed his eyes. 'No need. He went home yesterday.'

I never did get to see him.

As I backed out of Matt's room I bumped into Kerry on the landing. She was carrying a pile of tea towels.

'I'd like a word with you, young man.' She seemed angry. 'I had a visitor last night. Banging on my front door he was at half past eleven. But you'd know all about that, wouldn't you?'

'Was it Gabriel?' I asked.

'Who else? Did you put him up to it? Did you suggest he should come round to my house?'

'I thought … I thought you wanted to become an angel.'

She knelt down and took my hand. 'And you were right.'

Her face broke into a warm smile – she wasn't really angry, she was just pretending. I couldn't see a ring on her finger and I was worried Gabriel had messed everything up.

'Did he ask you?' I said.

'Ask? He went down on one knee and practically begged.' She kissed me on the cheek. 'Thanks, Sam.'

'So are you an angel now?'

'Nearly. We're going to see the vicar later on. All being well the big day will be ten weeks on Saturday.'

Then she was off, skipping down the stairs. 'Come on, you can give me a hand if you like.'

I helped Kerry get everything ready for breakfast. I checked all the salt and pepper pots were full and then put two sauce bottles, one brown and one red, on each table. A song was playing on the radio. 'Where's your mamma gone? Where's-your-*mamma*-gone? Far, far away!'

The words didn't hurt any more.

Kerry was practically dancing around the room arranging the napkins.

'Have you recovered from your adventure?' she asked.

'Yes, thanks,' I said.

I sat down at one of the tables.

'What happened to Hillary?' I asked. 'After he'd built the Tower.'

'For a while he carried on saving lives at sea, but eventually he had to admit he was an old man and he couldn't go on.'

Kerry poured some milk into all the little jugs and put one on each table.

'Towards the end of his life he'd become quite rich through his business interests and his dealings on the stock exchange,' she said. 'He lived in a fine house on Douglas Head from where he could see the sea. He had marvellous collections of paintings and antiques and if any man deserved to live out his last few years in comfort it was him, but it wasn't to be.'

'Why? What happened?'

'He was swindled by his business associates. Betrayed by those he thought he could trust.' Kerry sat down opposite me. 'He lost everything and was thrown out onto the streets. Some friends took him in and he spent his last days here on Mona Terrace.'

'Hillary lived here?'

'Only for a short while. He died soon afterwards. A broken man. He was buried in an old stone tomb with no inscription and just about forgotten.'

'But his grave is massive,' I said. 'I've seen it.'

'It is now,' said Kerry. 'It was only *after* his death that people fully appreciated what an incredible man he was. At the time there was no grand send-off for him. His was a sad and lonely passing.'

Kerry got to her feet and straightened the table-cloth.

'And that might have been the end of the story,' she said. 'But just as Hillary was remarkable in life, so he was in death.'

'What do you mean?'

'A few days after he'd been buried some people visit-
ed his tomb. It was open. The stone slab that had covered
the entrance had been moved. Hillary's body was gone.'

'How? Where?'

'Hillary died in debt,' explained Kerry. 'That meant
his body could have been sold for scientific purposes.
Some people believe that his friends went to the graveyard at night, removed his body and hid it to stop that
from happening.'

'Is that what you believe?'

'What other possible explanation is there?'

Kerry allowed me to bash the gong which meant I was
first to be seated for breakfast. The dining room soon
filled up, but she served me before anybody else.

A voice on the radio announced the local news head-
lines. 'The Douglas lifeboat was launched yesterday to
rescue two boys who had become cut off by the tide and
were stranded at the Tower of Refuge.'

Everybody in the dining room fell silent.

'The crew was alerted by a distress flare that was
spotted by a member of the public. The boys, who are
visitors to the island, were taken to Noble's Hospital, but
were suffering only from cold and exhaustion.'

'What about my ankle?' I said. 'Don't forget my ankle.'

Dad looked confused. 'What was all that about a distress flare?' He looked at the radio as if he was expecting
the announcer to answer him. 'Nobody fired a flare, did
they?'

The announcer ignored him and carried on with the
rest of the news.

Mr Fenton was staring at his plateful of sausages,
eggs and bacon. After a few minutes he banged his fists

on the table.

'To hell with it!' he shouted.

Everybody looked at him. We all watched as he pulled out his false teeth, wrapped them in his napkin and dived into his breakfast. He polished it off in two minutes flat and then asked Kerry for some more.

'You're hungry today,' she said.

'Hungry? I've not eaten anything since I got here because of my ruddy teeth!'

Mrs Fenton said she'd put on half a stone.

Suddenly Barney banged his fists on the table.

'To hell with it!' he shouted.

He held his wobbly tooth between finger and thumb, yanked it out, wrapped it in his napkin and tucked into his grub.

After breakfast Mrs Angel, Kerry and Gabriel gathered at the front door to say goodbye to us. Kerry gave each of us boys a hug and then Mrs Angel did the same.

'Bye, bye, my darlings,' she said. 'Come and see us again some time, won't you?'

'We certainly will,' said Dad. 'Thank you for everything.'

He turned to Kerry. 'And thank you too.' He put his hand in his pocket and took out some money. 'Here's a pound for you.' He handed it over awkwardly. 'It's a tip.'

'That's very kind,' said Kerry. 'Thank you.'

She kissed Dad on the cheek.

Matt gave me a nudge. 'I wonder what he'd have got for a fiver,' he whispered.

We walked down the garden path at Paradise House for the last time. At the gate I turned to have a final look at the house. On the patio Mrs Angel waved her hanky in the air. Gabriel waved and then he put his arm around

Kerry and she kissed him on the lips.

The taxi whisked us to the harbour where the *Manxman* was waiting for us. I led the way across the gangplank and we stood on her starboard side watching the sailors on the pier preparing to cast off. She gave three sharp blasts on her triple bell steam whistle. Dad told us it meant she was about to go astern and was warning any little boats to get out of her way. Sure enough we moved slowly backwards out of the harbour into the middle of the bay. The *Manxman* stopped and drifted silently on the water as if she was giving me a chance to have a last look at the Tower of Refuge standing on the rocks. Then I felt her engines power into life. We ran to the stern and watched the propellers churn the clear blue water into a frothy white foam. The *Manxman* moved forwards, turned hard to port and headed for home.

The sun was shining on the long row of brightly coloured hotels along the promenade. As we steamed further away it looked as if the sun was melting them. The colours slowly mixed together until they looked like a gigantic stick of seaside rock. We watched as the island became smaller and smaller until it was nothing more than a blur on the horizon. Then it was gone.

I reached out to hold Dad's hand. When I touched him he jumped as if I'd given him an electric shock, but then he took my hand in his. It felt strange at first. Mum's hand had been warm and soft. His was hard and cold. I realised it was the first time I'd ever held it.

chapter 32

Dad flicked open the catches of the suitcase, took out our dirty clothes and threw them into a heap in the middle of the living room floor.

'Back to reality,' he said.

He handed Barney his sandals.

'Take those outside please, they've got half of Douglas beach inside them.' He gave me the sandal that I'd rescued from the Tower. 'And you might as well chuck that away.'

'I want to keep it. Then I've got one and Davy Crockett's got one.'

'Who?'

'My other sandal is at the bottom of the sea. It's called Davy Crockett's locker.'

Dad smiled. 'It's Davy Jones's locker, not Davy Crockett's.'

'Who's Davy Jones?' I asked.

'I don't think anybody knows for sure,' said Dad. 'People reckon it's got something to do with that fella who got swallowed by a whale.'

'Pinocchio?' said Barney.

Dad laughed. 'No, the fella in the Bible.'

'Jonah,' I said.

'That's right.'

'But where does the locker bit come from? Is that

from the Bible too?'

'I don't know.'

'We'll ask Donald Duck on Sunday,' said Barney.

'Donald Duck?' said Dad.

'The vicar.'

Dad laughed again.

Me and Barney went into the yard and emptied our sandals. We poured the last few grains of our holiday into a little pyramid. When we went back into the kitchen Dad was twiddling the knobs on the washing machine. He looked a bit unsure.

'I'll show you how it works if you like,' I said. I lifted one of the two round lids. 'You put everything for washing in this tub and then you put them in the other one to spin and rinse. Keep well back though, when it's going full pelt it moves halfway across the kitchen. Once it trapped Barney against the wall!'

Dad stuffed the clothes into the machine.

'I'm hungry,' said Barney. 'What's for dinner?'

'Are we allowed to call it dinner?' I said. 'Or do we have to call it tea now that we're back home?'

'It doesn't matter what you call it,' said Dad. 'Because we haven't got anything.'

There was no food in the house and when Dad had started the washer he nipped to the grocer's to see what he could find.

Me, Matt and Barney set the table. We laid everything out just like at Paradise House – knife and fork with a soup spoon to one side and a dessert spoon at the top. Cup and saucer, sugar bowl, milk jug and teapot. (We didn't have a pot for hot water.)

'We haven't got any napkins,' said Barney.

Matt grabbed the box of paper tissues. 'Let's make some.'

We folded four of them neatly and placed them

between our knives and forks.

Dad came in the back door and told us to stay out of the kitchen because he was making a surprise. We took our seats at the table and after a short while Dad served our evening meal. It was beans on toast. *Triangular* toast!

Dad told us he'd made it by cutting ordinary bread from corner to corner.

'That was a lovely starter,' said Matt. 'What's for the main course?'

'And what's for dessert?' said Barney. 'I'd like fruit cocktail and cream, please.'

'You've had your taste of the high life,' said Dad. 'You're back in the real world now. Or at least you will be next week.'

'Why?' I asked. 'What's happening next week?'

'I'm going back to work.'

For a moment I was disappointed. Then I was shocked. Shocked that I'd felt disappointed because Dad wasn't going to be around all the time. He'd been like a different person while we were away. He'd hardly shouted, he hadn't hit us and he'd even tried to crack a few jokes. It must have been all the sea air he'd been breathing. Either that, or living with the angels for a few days.

After dinner me and Barney showed Dad and Matt our time capsule. We'd been planning to keep it a secret from them, but when Barney said he wanted to plant the Manx palm in Mum's little garden I thought we could bury our treasure beneath it.

We opened the biscuit tin and showed Dad and Matt our hoard. I asked Dad if he had anything to add to it. He emptied his pockets and gave us a few Manx coins and the tickets from our ride on the horse tram.

'Shall we put something of Mum's in it?' said Matt.

'Good idea,' said Barney.

He had a rummage in the cupboard under the stairs and pulled out the box of old photographs. He tipped them on to the floor, sifted through them and found the one of Mum with her mum and dad.

'What about this?'

'No,' said Dad. 'I don't think we should bury that. I think we should keep it.'

'Yeah,' said Matt. 'We could buy a frame for it.'

Barney put the photos back in the box. The one of Dad, the smiling sailor, was on the top.

'Why are there no photos of *your* mum and dad?' I asked.

'There are,' said Dad.

He took an old cigar box out of a sideboard drawer. Inside was a bundle of photos. He handed one of them to me. It was a picture of a lady in her Sunday best.

'Is that your mum?'

He nodded.

'Did she die?'

'Yes. When I was thirteen.'

'What was her name?' I asked.

'Agnes.'

Dad handed me another photograph. A man dressed in overalls was sitting on a wall.

'Is that your dad?'

'Yes.'

'What was his name?'

'Archie.'

'Did he die as well?'

'When I was four. I never really knew him. I can only remember what he looked like because of that photo.'

'That would be weird,' said Matt. 'If you never knew your Dad.'

'What are these?' Barney was rummaging in the

cigar box. 'Medals?'

Dad nodded.

'Are they yours?' said Matt.

Dad nodded again.

'Nice one.'

Barney flicked through the other photos. 'Who are these sailors? Look at the size of that ship! Have you been on it, Dad?'

'We can look at those later,' said Dad. 'Let's get the palm planted before it goes dark.'

'We haven't put anything of Mum's in the time capsule,' said Barney.

'I've got something,' I said.

I went upstairs and fetched the tin of talcum powder.

Barney held it to his nose. 'It smells like Mum.'

He placed it in the tin. Meantime Matt had written a note:

If ye have found this buried treasure,
Ye may keep it and good luck we say,
But never harm Mum's palm tree,
Or ye will be cursed for ever and a day.

He deliberately spilled some cold tea on the piece of paper and burned the corners with Dad's cigarette lighter. He made it look like a pirate's scroll. It was brilliant. He rolled it up and placed it in the tin.

I got the trowel from under the kitchen sink and we went into the yard. Dad hitched up his sleeves and dug into Mum's little garden. (I made sure he wasn't near Coconut's grave.)

'The ground is very wet,' he said. 'I don't think we should bury the treasure here. The damp will get into the tin and spoil everything.'

'Where can we bury it?' said Barney.

'I'll find somewhere in a minute. Let's get this in

first.'

Dad carefully lifted the baby palm out of its pot and placed it in the hole. He flattened the earth around it with his hands and then clapped them together to shake off the bits of soil.

The four of us stood for a moment and gazed at the little palm in our garden of remembrance.

'Mum would have liked that,' said Matt.

'Yeah,' said Dad. 'I'm sure she would.'

'Let's bury the treasure,' said Barney.

We followed Dad down the yard. He tapped the trowel on one of the paving stones on the path.

'Open Sesame!' he said.

Then he pushed the trowel down the side of the paving stone and lifted the whole thing out. Underneath was a hole about a foot deep.

'Wow!' said Barney. 'A secret place!'

'How did you know it was there, Dad?' asked Matt.

'It's where the tap for the water mains used to be, but it was disconnected years ago.' Dad reached into the hole. 'Dry as a bone down here.'

'Perfect,' I said.

Dad put the tin in the hole and replaced the paving stone.

'It'll be a while before anybody finds that,' he said.

'Yeah,' said Barney. 'And when they do they'll find the note about Mum's palm tree and then they'll know all about it.'

That's when I realised that nobody would ever really know anything unless I told them. That's when I decided to write everything down and secretly add it to the time capsule without the others knowing.

Dad and Matt went back into the house.

'Shall we water the palm tree?' said Barney.

'No need,' I said. 'It looks as if it's going to rain.'

Barney was staring at the palm as if he was expecting it to start growing there and then.

'I bet we're the only people round here with a bit of heaven on earth in their back yard,' he said.

We sat on the path and chatted until the rain began to fall. We talked about our trip, the angels and everything that had happened.

Mum was there with us, of course. And she always will be. Wherever we are, whatever we're doing, she will always be by our side.